"Already?" She frowned faintly. "Here or the motel, huh?"

"Well, I have a guest room if you'd rather. No problem for me."

The offer was out before he knew it was coming, and then Matthew seconded it. The idea of having someone new in the house seemed to appeal to him.

Vanessa's hesitation seemed obvious. Matthew was already running on about how they could read his library book together, but she had drawn away. He could feel it. Pulled back into herself.

"Look," he said finally. "I'll guide you to the motel if you want, but like I said, mostly truckers and transients stay there. This house is okay if you want to stock it up. I was only thinking about you being here alone if the blizzard gets bad. You'd be stuck, and the phones aren't working."

He could swear she felt torn in a bunch of different directions. But then she surprised him.

"If you're sure I won't put you out..."

That settled it, he decided. A night or two. As soon as she'd made her decisions about the house, she'd drive away.

Matthew was ecstatic. Tim watched him with a faint smile, but once again reflected on how much that boy must miss having a mother. He hoped a couple of days wasn't long enough for him to fit Vanessa into that role.

CONARD COUNTY: THE NEXT GENERATION

Dear Reader,

When I was a child, I moved a lot. The first move I remember was when I was four, and the next one happened before I turned seven. Until high school, my father's job obliged us to move every two years...or if we managed to stay a little longer something required me to change schools and meet a whole new group of peers.

I never thought what that might be doing to me. I hated the moves; I hated having to start all over again, but that was the way it was. I couldn't imagine what it was like for people I met who'd grown up with their friends. At the time, my only thought was that they had a different life.

When I became an adult, I realized I was a nomad. Come springtime, I always wanted to move. Of course, that was impractical, but it was years before I realized how my childhood had shaped me: I couldn't create enduring, deep friendships. Everything was superficial, and my heart remained forever ready to move on.

Vanessa is facing the same problem, but Tim helps her to surmount it. She learns to truly open her heart.

Happy reading,

Rachel Lee

A Conard County Courtship

———

Rachel Lee

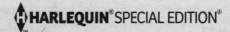

Recycling programs
for this product may
not exist in your area.

ISBN-13: 978-0-373-62375-4

A Conard County Courtship

Copyright © 2017 by Susan Civil Brown

This edition published by arrangement with Harlequin Books S.A.

For questions and comments about the quality of this book, please contact us at CustomerService@Harlequin.com.

Printed in U.S.A.

Rachel Lee was hooked on writing by the age of twelve and practiced her craft as she moved from place to place all over the United States. This *New York Times* bestselling author now resides in Florida and has the joy of writing full-time.

Visit the Author Profile page
at Harlequin.com for more titles

Chapter One

She never expected to find a man in the house. Vanessa Welling stood on the wet sidewalk between two low banks of melting snow and looked at the house she owned but didn't want. The hatred and pain that rose in her had been planted nearly twenty years ago by the man who had lived in that house, the man who had destroyed her family, and she'd like to set a match to the whole place.

She'd tried to get out of it, had argued with the lawyer who had called her to tell her it belonged to her. Unfortunately, Bob Higgins had deeded it over to her before he died in prison, and the really odd thing—to her, at least—was that he was free to do that even if she didn't want it. She couldn't refuse it. She couldn't give it back, and right now she was responsible for the taxes on the place. She would remain responsible for them and any code violations or fines until she managed to dump it.

Her stomach burned, her eyes felt hot in her head and everything she had tried to bury was rising sickeningly inside her.

Had that man thought this was some kind of atonement? Because it wasn't. No house could give her back her father or the years lost to his alcoholism. No house could give her back everything else that had been ripped from her at a tender age, wounding her in ways that remained with her.

She had never wanted to see this town again. She remembered how her father felt the people here must be judging him, thinking him a fool for having lost his ranch and every bit of savings to Bob Higgins. His bitterness had branded itself in Vanessa's heart, and her mother hadn't done much to erase it. Belinda Welling had been quieter in her response, but despair had filled her days. Her husband's alcoholism had overwhelmed her, and Vanessa felt that in many ways she had had to raise herself.

Now here she was, owner of the house that had belonged to the beast who had destroyed everything, and she had to at least see to fixing it up enough that she could sell it. Get rid of it. Remove any demand that she ever return here.

The street was quiet, but it was early on a Monday afternoon. Kids in school, parents at work and weather less than hospitable.

The key in her hand felt acidic, hot, as if it would eat a hole in her palm. She wanted to fling it into the snow.

Just get it done, she told herself. Just walk in there, face the memories that lurked and would probably pounce to remind her that this had once been a favorite place of hers to visit. She'd arrange whatever needed to be done, then get the hell out of this town before the whispers started, before people began to ask each other if that was Milt Welling's daughter and hadn't he been a fool to trust that Higgins guy with everything he owned?

As she walked up toward the porch, freshly laid salt crunching beneath her feet, she felt a sharp gust of icy wind. After twenty years she had no intuitive understanding of the weather around her, but to her that gust spoke of an approaching snowstorm, as did the clattering of leafless branches on the trees that lined the street.

Or maybe she was imagining it. Why not? She was walking toward the door of a house that had populated her nightmares. All that was missing was some spooky, threatening music.

How over the top could she go, she wondered as she leveled the key at the lock and felt a small burst of self-amusement puncture her anger and apprehension. Bob, the man who had ruined her family, was dead. He couldn't hurt her anymore. And leaving her his house? Probably his final laugh at someone else's expense, not an attempt to atone at all. That would fit.

It wasn't as if he hadn't stolen money from anyone else. He'd just stolen more from her father. As in everything.

Just as she turned the key in the lock, the door opened and she stood face-to-face with a tall man wearing a khaki work shirt, dusty jeans, work boots and a loaded tool belt slung around narrow hips. His eyes were the same gray as the leaden sky above, his face perfectly chiseled and showing some faint smile lines around his mouth and crinkles at the corners of his eyes. His dark brown hair was tousled and dusty. *Um, wow?*

"Hi," he said, his voice deep and pleasant. "Something I can help you with?"

Well, this was totally unexpected. This was *her* house, yet there was a stranger in it. Could he help her? But then her memory kicked in. Hadn't the lawyer said something about sending someone to look over the condition of the house?

She found her voice at last. "I'm Vanessa Welling. Who are you?"

His dark eyebrows lifted, then he smiled. "Ah. I guess Earl didn't tell you he'd hired me to check out the place, and he told me he didn't expect you before the weekend. I'm Tim Dawson. I'm a building contractor— Earl sent me. If you want, I can wait outside while you look around. Or just come back another day."

Why should he do that? But then she realized he must think that she might be uncomfortable about entering an empty house occupied by a man she'd never met before. She ought to be, but strangely she wasn't. Anyway, if anyone should leave, it ought to be her. She didn't want to be here at all.

The door still wide-open, both of them poised to leave, Vanessa shook her head a little and thought that her life had turned into a series of vignettes written by someone else from the minute Earl had told her she'd inherited this house. Nothing had run in its usual course since then.

"No," she said. "You're working. Frankly, I'd be happy never to see the inside of this place."

"I heard from Earl you didn't want it. That stinks." He stepped back, giving her space to enter if she chose. "It always bothered me that someone could just deed a property to someone else even if they don't want it. Never understood that one."

"I'm still trying to wrap my brain around it." Hesitantly, she stepped through the door into the wide foyer. It had once been an elegant house, but it had been a long time since anyone had lived here. Some of the wallpaper was peeling. "How bad is it?"

"The place got winterized before the previous owner…left, so there's surprisingly little damage to important stuff. Plumbing still works, in other words. No broken pipes. Right now I'm finishing up work on the heater to see if I can get it operating again. It's an old model, but I don't imagine you even want to consider a new one."

"Not if I can help it. I don't want to live here, I just want to get to the point where I can get rid of it without having tax liens and code violations follow me through life."

"I can see that. Well, I was just going out to my truck to get a valve, so take a look around. I'll be happy to answer any questions I can."

She watched him walk out the door, thinking that it was criminal that a man that good-looking had walked into her life in the last place on earth she wanted to be.

She watched him cross the street to a white truck with small lettering on the side. That explained why she'd never guessed someone would be in here.

Then she forced herself to turn and face the inside of the house. To face memories that should have been good but had turned to ash.

* * *

Vanessa Welling was a pretty woman, Tim thought as he crossed the wet street and opened a compartment on the side of his pickup. Maybe more than pretty, but since she was clearly unhappy at the moment he couldn't be really sure. Right now, she was simply a catalog of externalities: auburn hair, mossy-green eyes, a bit on the tiny side.

Earl Carter, father of the local judge, was a font of history when it came to this county, especially the ugly legal parts. The story of how Bob Higgins had managed to rob the Welling family blind was the stuff of novels or movies…except according to Earl, this kind of thing happened all the time. Con men, con jobs—and the Wellings hadn't been the only ones robbed. Apparently, a number of others had fallen for Higgins's financial planning business, to their detriment, but only the Wellings had lost more than a retirement fund.

Sad story. Vanessa would have been a kid when it all happened, but from what Earl had said, she remembered enough to be filled with loathing. Imagine inheriting the house of the man who had ruined your family. Tim couldn't make up his mind if Higgins had been diabolical or regretful.

Anyway, Vanessa had a problem to deal with, and he'd bet she wanted to make her decisions and get the hell out of Conard County as fast as she could.

Shame, because he'd like to get a chance to know the woman behind that haunted, heart-shaped face. Not that it mattered, really. Just a reaction to a new face. He had his hands full enough raising a seven-year-old boy whose mother had died. A change of pace might be nice, but it would be transitory.

He was just crossing the street again with the valve he wanted in hand when a black Cadillac pulled up. It was an older car, kept in scrupulously good shape by its owner, Earl Carter. Earl pulled up against the curb on the far side of the street and rolled his window down. "She's here?"

"Oh, yeah."

"I just got her message." Earl, a pleasantly plump man who was awfully popular around town for a lawyer, shook his head faintly. "Sorry, I didn't think she would be here so soon."

"It's not a problem. But she's clearly not happy to be here."

"No kidding. I'm sorry I couldn't find her a way out. Is she inside?"

"Yeah. I just came out to get a valve for a gas line."

"I'll go in with you. Two strange men in one day might be too much."

Tim almost laughed. They would still be two strange men in the otherwise empty house with her. Hardly likely to make her feel easier, except that Earl slightly resembled a teddy bear. The years and some beer had given him a bit of a belly and softened his face. He looked kindly by nature.

"Well, come on, but she was looking as if she wanted to burn the place down."

"Probably does," Earl said, climbing out. He might be the last man in town who wore a business suit routinely. Even his own son, the judge, often wore jeans under his judicial robes.

"Let me call inside first," Tim suggested. "Let her know we're both here. This can't be easy for her."

"It's not," Earl said. "Not at all. Bet she hits the road just as quick as she can."

"Maybe." He wasn't about to predict what anyone else would do. Dangerous game, that.

"She didn't want this place," Earl mused, pausing on the walk before heading for the porch. "She may change her mind, though. With a little work, this house will become prime real estate. Great location, good size. She should make a pretty penny if she shapes it up."

"Sure, we sell so much prime real estate around here." Tim's tone was dry. Given the kind of work he did, he knew how sluggish the market was locally. Nothing new for this town. Boom or bust. Right now, it was more bust.

"Cut it out, boy," Earl said. "We'll get that ski resort and this house would make a good bed-and-breakfast."

"Now that's prime optimism," Tim answered. "That ski resort has been a pipe dream forever. I'd bet the landslide finished the idea, even if Luke is back to checking the geology for a developer."

"Someone's paying him," was Earl's answer. "So someone is interested in doing it."

Someone had been interested in the possibility of a resort on the mountainside Tim's entire adult life. So far nothing had been done beyond clearing a few ski trails, a small investment in downtown improvement with brick sidewalks and Victorian lampposts, and a survey of the hotel site. Then the landslide. Tim just shook his head and wondered if being an eternal optimist was part of how people survived around here. He tended to lean toward optimism himself, despite everything. He had a kid to think about.

"Let's get going," he said. "I need to finish work on the heater in time to go pick my son up."

Earl glanced at him. "He doesn't walk home?"

"Not when a blizzard is in the forecast." Tim nodded toward the sky. "Rapid temperature drop this afternoon. Whiteout conditions."

"You don't say. I should pay more attention, I guess."

Tim smiled as they climbed the porch steps and he opened the door. Earl was a gadabout when he wasn't being a damn good lawyer. Why would he pay attention to the weather report? He could get to his son's house or Mahoney's to have beer with friends. Unless court dates had to be postponed, the effects of bad weather on Earl would be minimal.

Opening the door and leaning in, Tim called out, "Ms. Welling? It's me, Tim, and I've brought your lawyer with me. Earl Carter."

As he and Earl crossed the threshold, he heard hurried footsteps from the back of the house. Still wearing her jacket, with her hands stuffed in her pockets, Vanessa managed a smile.

"So you're Earl Carter."

"One and the same." Earl smiled. "Lots of time on the phone, but nothing like face-to-face." He stuck out his hand, and Vanessa freed hers to shake it. "Well, what do you think?"

"About the house? Besides the fact I don't want it? It needs work, Earl. I supposed Mr. Dawson knows how sound it is generally, but paint is sagging on some of the walls. Sagging! I don't think I've ever seen that before."

"Bad paint job," Tim remarked. "Old paint. Lack of care. Nothing that can't be fixed."

"This place looks like a headache," she said frankly. "I wish you could have stopped Bob Higgins from doing this to me."

Earl shook his head. "He did this all on his own. I never knew about it until he died. Then everything landed on my desk."

"It landed on me like a ton of bricks," she said. "I never wanted to come back here. Never."

Tim decided it might be a good time to step out of the conversation. "I need to go put this valve on the heater so I can get it up and running again. It's getting cold in here. There's a pot of coffee in the kitchen. Why don't you two help yourselves?"

He headed down to the basement, acutely aware that without heat, given the coming cold, this place could suffer a lot of damage now that he'd turned on the plumbing again. Eventually that heater should be replaced, but he had a feeling Vanessa Welling wouldn't be the one to do it.

In the chilly kitchen with Earl Carter, Vanessa pulled out a chair and sat at a table she remembered all too well.

"Bet you remember this house," Earl remarked.

"I don't want to talk about it." She really didn't. Good memories had been turned into a nightmare by the man who had inflicted this house on her, and she had little desire to look back.

"You used to play with the Higgins kids, didn't you?"

She looked at him. "I think I said I didn't want to talk about it."

"You did," he acknowledged. "But I don't want to talk about your memories. That was a lead-in to how you're sitting here. After Bob Higgins was arrested, his wife took their two kids and left. I got to wondering why she didn't sell the house at some point, then I learned why. She never owned it. It was his, lock, stock and barrel."

"That fits," Vanessa said tautly. The guy didn't even take care of his family. He'd made sure everything was his, even their house.

"So, anyway, I only looked into it to find out how it had come to you. When you said you didn't want it, I hunted his ex-wife up and suggested that you might be willing to give it to her. She was as interested as you were. Didn't want to even think about it. So here we are."

"So he ruined everyone's lives."

"That's how it looks. She's remarried. Even changed the last name of the children."

Vanessa nodded slightly and looked down as Earl put a mug of coffee in front of her. That looked better than anything she'd seen since arriving here. Well, except for Tim Dawson. "I hate this, Earl," she said, reaching out to grip the mug in both hands for its warmth.

"No better man than Tim Dawson to take care of it for you. He'll be quick, he won't overcharge and he won't do more than you want and need him to do."

She raised her gaze to his. "But what about selling it?"

"We'll get that done somehow, too. We haven't got the busiest real estate market, but a house like this, reasonably priced, should sell. And you can afford to price it reasonably, because your only sunk costs are going to be for basic repairs and taxes."

She hadn't thought about that, and it made her feel slightly better. She could sell it for a song, then it wouldn't be her problem anymore. Or maybe she could even find a place to donate it, once she was sure it was safe. A house left basically abandoned for twenty years might have all kinds of safety problems. No termites, though, according to Earl. That had been the first thing he had checked out.

So…it would be okay, she told herself yet again. Lately that had become a mantra.

Earl let her have some silence, for which she was grateful. She was still trying to deal with the mess of emotions coming back here had awakened in her. She had a lot to be angry about, a lot to be sad about, and feelings she had put away long ago had all surfaced with her return, with having to deal with this house.

The past had become present, through no choice of her own, and for the first time she considered just how much she hadn't been able to get over. No, it seemed more like she had plastered over all the cracks and the plaster was giving way. She'd even started having bad dreams again.

Some things were better left buried, and she wished all of this had remained in its grave. What the hell had Bob Higgins been thinking? He'd had no conscience about robbing her family into abject poverty. Why would he have gotten one at such a late stage in his life?

Chilly air stirred suddenly, and she heard a distant *whoompf* that probably indicated Tim had started the heater. Considering that he had the water running now, that was an excellent thing.

A minute later he appeared, wiping his hands on a

rag that he jammed into the back pocket of his jeans. "All set. They make much more efficient models now, but this will do. It shouldn't break down, anyway. And when you're ready to go, I'll winterize the house again."

He grabbed some coffee of his own and joined her at the table.

"I was just getting ready to leave," Earl announced. "I have a three o'clock meeting. If you need anything, call me." He handed her a business card along with a warm smile, then walked out.

When Vanessa remained silent, Tim spoke. "I guess this hit you like a ton of bricks."

"To put it mildly."

He just shook his head, unsure what he could say. "I've got to run soon as well. I need to pick up my son from school. I'll bring him back here so we can have some time to discuss what has to be done and whether you want to do any more than that."

She nodded. "How old is your son?"

"Seven. Anyway, we're going to be getting a sharp temperature drop anytime now, and I don't want him out there walking in subzero temps."

"I'd forgotten." If she'd ever really known. "It can change fast, can't it?"

"Very fast. And we're just sliding into winter, so nobody's really ready. Blizzard tonight, maybe. If you can stand it, you might want to stay here rather than at the motel. We can get you some food in so you don't have to hoof it or drive to get a meal. The thing about the motel is that it's used mainly by truckers and transients. You might feel safer here, much as you hate it."

"I'll think about it."

He stood. "I'll be back in fifteen or twenty minutes… unless you'd rather I didn't come back."

For once since getting here she didn't feel like hesitating. "No, come back. I'd like to meet your son."

He nodded once with a smile, then left the kitchen. She listened to his boots cross the foyer, then the front door opened and closed.

Earl had done his best, Tim was a nice guy and maybe she could survive this trip after all.

But the thought of being snowed in here? She shuddered. There'd be no way to avoid the memories then.

From what Earl had told him, Tim guessed this visit had to be a painful one for Vanessa. Although she'd been a child his own son's age when her family's life had fallen apart, she probably remembered enough to find it uncomfortable to return. While it was old news, when Bob Higgins had died in prison, people had recalled his life and crimes, and inevitably Tim had learned something about the man.

He'd apparently set himself up as an investment adviser and had a few impressive pieces of paper framed on his office wall. He'd even been licensed by the state. Everyone knew him, most people liked him and it hadn't taken him long to get his business rolling.

It must have rolled well for ten or twelve years before it caught up with him. Tim didn't understand exactly how the scheme had worked, but Bob had persuaded people to entrust him with their money to invest, and most had only given him amounts they never needed back, or if they needed to pull something out, they'd been able to.

But Vanessa's parents had been different. They'd thought their investments were growing so well that Bob Higgins had managed to persuade them to give him even more, promising them a fortune. They'd mortgaged their ranch and had learned the bleak truth when they needed money from their investments to pay that mortgage.

Tim didn't pretend to understand how it all had worked or why Higgins had persuaded the Wellings to mortgage their ranch. Maybe because he was getting to the point where he needed money to pay clients a return?

Regardless of it all, the Wellings had left town, and Bob Higgins had been exposed and sent to jail.

But he could see no earthly reason why the man would have deeded his house to Vanessa. No *good* reason.

He joined the line of parents waiting in their vehicles at the elementary school. The temperature had begun to drop, and the teachers were blowing clouds of fog when they spoke and hurried the children along. Cheeks quickly brightened to red, and there was little of the usual horseplay. The cold had shocked the kids, too.

Tim started to smile as he watched his son, Matthew, race toward the truck. The boy reminded him of his mother, Claire, with his round face, a splatter of freckles across his nose, and a dark blond hair. Every time Tim saw him, he felt an ache for Claire.

Leaning over, he unlatched the door and threw it open for the boy. Matt scrambled in then used both hands to close the door. As usual, Matt did everything at top speed.

The door was open long enough, however, for Tim

to feel the dangerous cold deepening outside. If the forecast held, they might need to close school tomorrow. Occasionally it grew too cold to expect children to walk to school or to bus stops.

"How was your day, kiddo?"

"Okay," Matthew answered. He grinned as he struggled to buckle himself in, showing off the two new front teeth that were emerging. He'd just outgrown the child seat, but was still having trouble with the regular seat belt.

"Just okay?" Tim asked.

"Well, Orson turned green around his neck and got all ruffed up." Orson was an exotic lizard who lived in a large aquarium. "Ms. Macy said something must have scared him. That was probably Tommy. He kept banging a penny against the tank."

"Why did Tommy do that?"

Matthew shrugged. "I guess it was fun. Everybody was pretty mad about Orson, though. He doesn't bother anybody."

"I don't imagine he does. Lots of homework?"

"Not much. Two work sheets."

At last able to pull out of the line, Tim drove back toward the Higgins house—although he supposed it was the Welling house now—and listened to Matthew's cheerful recounting of the day and his pride in bringing home his very first library book from the school.

It wasn't as if Tim hadn't been taking him to the public library all along, but the school library was something special.

"Where are we going, Daddy?"

"Back to the house I'm working on. There's a lady there now—she owns the house. So…"

"Company manners," Matthew said with a sharp nod of his head. "Is she a nice lady?"

"I think so, but I just met her before I came to get you."

"She's not a witch?" Matt asked, scrunching up his face and making his small hands into claws.

"What *have* you been reading?" Tim asked, eliciting a giggle.

"Fun stuff. Ms. Macy says I'm too young for Harry Potter, though."

"Oh. Did you want to read it?" He suspected Ms. Macy's objection arose more from what some parents around here thought of children reading about wizards and magic.

"Joey's brother did. He loves it."

"Well, I'll see what I can do about getting a copy from the library. You can try it and see."

For that he received an ear-to-ear grin.

Occasionally when he talked with his son, Tim felt a nostalgia for his own childhood, when everything had been simple and magical. Other times, though, when Matt was having a problem of some kind, Tim was more than glad to be so much older. He suspected that feeling would grow when Matthew hit his teens.

This time he pulled up right in front of the house. Vanessa had parked in the narrow driveway, so there didn't seem to be any reason to leave curb space. Especially with the temperature dropping so rapidly.

Matthew started to pull his backpack out with him, and Tim stopped him. "You won't need that until we get home."

"But I want to show the new lady my library book!"

Tim let him go but wondered if Vanessa would be pleasant, bored or annoyed. Matthew wasn't her child, after all, and for all he knew she had little patience for youngsters. Still, how annoyed could she be over a library book?

"Company manners," he reminded Matthew as they walked toward the front door.

"I know, Dad." The boy's tone was a touch exasperated, making Tim smile faintly. How fast they tried to grow up.

Vanessa was still sitting in the kitchen with her coffee. Apparently she'd felt no urge to explore the house. Sooner or later, she would have to do a walk-through with him. He could understand her being angry with Higgins, but the house? No, she hadn't wanted it, but surely she didn't have anything against the house. It was an inanimate object.

"Ms. Welling, this is my son, Matthew."

She had lifted her head at the approach of their footsteps, and now she managed a faint smile. "Hello, Matthew. If you want, you can call me Vannie."

"Vannie?" he repeated as if memorizing it. "I got a new library book. Wanna see?"

Kids, thought Tim. They got through the rough spots as if they weren't there, skipped over the awkwardness of first meetings and just accepted everyone as a friend.

"I'd love to see," she answered. Her expression remained pleasant and her tone neutral. Okay, she'd be polite.

"We can't take too long, Matthew. Vannie's going to need to get some groceries before the snow starts."

He looked at Vanessa. "The cold out there will snatch your breath."

"Already?" She frowned faintly. "Here or the motel, huh?"

"Well, I have a guest room, if you'd rather. No problem for me."

The offer was out before he knew it was coming, and then Matthew seconded it. The idea of having someone new in the house seemed to appeal to him.

Vanessa's hesitation appeared obvious. Matthew was already running on about how they could read his library book together, but she had drawn away. He could feel it. Pulled back into herself.

"Look," he said finally. "I'll guide you to the motel if you want, but like I said, mostly truckers and transients stay there. This house is okay if you want to stock it up. I was only thinking about you being here alone if the blizzard gets bad. You'd be stuck, and the phones here aren't working. Cell phones can become unreliable when the air's full of blowing snow."

He could have sworn she felt torn in a bunch of different directions. But then she surprised him.

"If you're sure I won't put you out..."

That settled it, he decided. A night or two. As soon as she'd made her decisions about the house, she'd drive away.

Matthew was ecstatic. Tim watched him with a faint smile, but once again reflected on how much that boy must miss having a mother. He hoped a couple of days wasn't long enough for him to fit Vanessa into that role.

Chapter Two

Vanessa hoped she hadn't made a mistake. Tim Dawson seemed like a laid-back sort of guy, however attractive, and his son was a trip. It ought to be okay for a few days.

But honestly, the thought of being stuck alone in Bob Higgins's house because of a blizzard had been more than she could face. As she'd sat there, waiting for Tim to return with his son, memories had clamored, and maybe the worst part was that they were so confused.

So much for thinking she'd dealt with the past and put it away. The house had dug it all up again. It would have been okay if the memories had been bad, but the thing was, they were good memories, which made Bob Higgins's betrayal all that more difficult to deal with.

When she stepped outside to follow Tim to his house,

the icy air astonished her. The temperature had fallen that fast? She wore what she'd thought would be an adequate wool coat, but it wasn't enough.

She hurried to get into her car and out of the wind. Matthew had told his father he wanted to ride with her, but before she could say anything Tim had squashed that. Good. She liked the kid as much as she could, having only just met him, but she was far from being ready to drive him around. Also, she knew next to nothing about children.

Maybe she should have gone to the motel. The town had only one, it seemed, and the reviews hadn't been exciting. Truckers and transients? And what if she got snowed in there?

She shook her head at herself. She wasn't usually a ditherer, but then she'd never faced a situation quite like this before. Not as an adult making her own decisions.

A town she had nearly forgotten that held secrets about her family that might cause people to judge her. Her dad had certainly thought so. A house from the man who'd destroyed her family. She couldn't imagine staying there by herself to deal with the good memories that refused to jibe with later reality. Worse, the bad memories from later were more sharply engraved on her mind. She didn't want to relive her dad's deterioration and death. All that bitterness. Her mother's despair.

She hoped Bob Higgins had gone to hell, then caught herself. She didn't wish that on anyone. But that was the problem with being back here. Having thoughts like that. She was going to face a very ugly part of herself until she was able to walk away.

Tim lived right around the corner. He pulled into a

paved driveway that left enough room for her to pull in beside him. She was relieved she wouldn't be blocking him in or leaving her car on the street to interfere with snowplows.

From the outside, the two-story house appeared tidy—freshly painted white, black shutters all in good condition. A side door led into a mudroom, and from there into a warmly decorated kitchen, painted yellow with sunflower decals along the soffits. A woman's touch.

"Your wife won't mind?" she asked, a belated concern. It almost embarrassed her that she hadn't asked earlier.

"I'm widowed," Tim said as he bent to give Matthew a friendly pat on his behind and sent him to put his backpack away. "Homework before dinner."

"Okay, Dad, but I still haven't showed Vannie my book."

"After the work sheets are done, okay? She'd probably like to put her suitcase in the spare room and settle a bit."

Matthew looked at Vanessa and grinned. "I don't have much homework."

"Then I'll have to hurry my settling in."

Matthew dashed off, leaving Tim and Vanessa alone for a moment.

"He's cute," Vanessa offered.

"He's also endlessly energetic. Don't let him bug you too much. Come on, I'll show you your room."

Miserable as she had been by herself at the Higgins house, now she felt a desperate need for a few minutes alone. With her emotions all topsy-turvy, she needed just a little time to let them settle.

Closing the door behind her in the guest room seemed like a sure way to get that done. Tim brought in her suitcase, told her where to find the facilities, then left her alone in a lovely room.

She suspected he cherished the memory of his wife, because little enough had been done to erase a woman's touch. No man had chosen those white ruffled curtains or thought to put an embroidered oval doily on the top of the mirrored dresser. A comforter decorated with forget-me-nots covered the queen-size bed, and matching rugs scattered the polished wood floor.

Definitely his wife's choices, she thought, along with the pale lavender paint on the walls.

So he hadn't changed a thing. That told her something about his grief. Then she thought of his son, the boy without a mother, and reluctantly her heart went out to them both. The fact that she didn't make relationships didn't mean she didn't care.

It was the relationships that could frighten her. But for Tim and Matthew…that wasn't enough to unnerve her. She didn't intend to be here that long.

She enjoyed a few minutes by herself, changing out of her traveling clothes into more comfortable green fleece, pants and thick socks. Then she decided it was time to go out and face the world of Tim and Matthew. Hanging around in her room might seem rude to Tim after he'd been awfully nice to invite her to stay here.

As she passed the dining room, she saw Matthew hunkered over some papers, chewing on a pencil. He flashed her a grin and went back to work.

She found Tim in the kitchen, washing and patting

down a whole chicken. "Can I help?" she offered automatically.

"No need. Just have a seat at the kitchen table. Coffee?"

"No, thank you. Maybe some water?"

"There are bottles in the fridge, and glasses in the cabinet beside it if you want one. I'm a bottle drinker, I'm afraid. Anyway, apologies for not getting it for you, but my hands are covered with chicken."

"I don't expect to be waited on," she assured him. "It's kind of you to give me shelter from the storm. Honestly, I didn't want to stay alone at the house, and Earl's and your description of the motel made me uneasy."

Tim nodded as he placed the chicken in the roasting pan beside the sink. "You'd probably be okay there, but you aren't going to want to have to cross the highway in a blizzard this cold just to get to the truck stop to eat something. Anyway, with this weather moving in, they'll be packed...and so will the truck stop diner." He flashed her a smile. "My house is so much nicer."

"It is," she agreed readily. "Your spare room is beautiful. Your wife?"

"Yeah."

She watched him oil the chicken then wash his hands again, wondering if mention of his wife was off-limits.

When he was done prepping the chicken, he washed his hands again then leaned back against the counter as he dried them with a towel. "My wife passed six years ago. Pulmonary embolism, if you can believe it. Out of nowhere. Matthew has absolutely no memory of her. I can't decide if that's good or bad."

"I wouldn't know," she said carefully. "I am very sorry for your loss."

He tossed the towel to one side. "You get used to the most incredible things. Anyway, yeah, she decorated most of the house. Your room was her pride, though. It wasn't often she could find everything she wanted that would match." He rested his palms on the counter behind him. "What about you?"

"Me?"

"People you're in a hurry to get back to?"

"I work at a natural history museum, and they told me to take whatever time I needed." Indeed, they'd been very kind. But she was also acutely aware that she hadn't answered his questions. He'd been straightforward with her, and she felt she needed to give him something in kind.

"My parents are both dead, and there's no one else." And never would be. No risks of that nature. She'd seen the price up close and personal, as they said.

He didn't press the issue but instead turned to pop the chicken in the oven when something beeped. "We eat early around here. Better for Matthew. Tonight we'll have broccoli with cheese and boxed stuffing to go with this. I hope that sounds good."

"It sounds great."

He got himself a bottle of water from the fridge. She still hadn't gotten one for herself, so he placed one in front of her with a glass.

"So what do you do at the museum?" he asked.

"I help connect dinosaur bones. Unfortunately, they're rarely discovered as a complete kit. Weather, erosion, what have you, have scattered and mixed the bones. So my job is to figure out what they are and which ones belong where."

"Do you assemble them?"

She shook her head. "Not unless there's an extraordinary find. No, mostly we catalog and put them away for safekeeping and later study. It's not like we know everything."

"Matt would probably love a trip to see dinosaur bones."

She smiled. "I'm sure he would. And this summer there'll probably be several digs going on around this state. Wyoming is a great place for fossil beds. He could see someone pulling them out of the ground...if he has the patience."

"I've read about that. Just never thought about taking the time. Guess I should."

A silence fell, and she felt awkward about it. With people she knew, silences could be allowed, but she didn't know this man that well. "You don't have to entertain me," she nearly blurted.

He lifted one corner of his mouth in a half smile. "That goes both ways. Besides, once he finishes his homework, Matthew will take over the entertaining. You'll probably be begging to go to your room for some solitude."

A laugh trickled out of her. "I've hardly met him, but he seems high energy."

"I've often wished we could tap some of that energy for ourselves as we get older. It's amazing. He can wear me out sometimes."

"All kids are like that, right?"

"I would worry if one weren't." He glanced at his

watch. "Want to move into the living room? I've got an hour before I need to start the rest of dinner. We could check in on how bad the storm will be."

She was agreeable and followed him into another tasteful room. His wife was a living presence here, she realized. In a good way. She had created a comfortable, lovely home.

He flipped on the wide-screen TV to the weather station. Whatever else had been in the programming had given way to a nearly breathless description of the storm that bore down on them, complete with advice not to travel and to stay inside if possible.

"These are going to be killer temperatures," the woman reciting the weather said. "Not a time to decide to make snowballs, kids, or a snowman. You could leave your fingers behind."

"Or worse," Tim said. "Do you remember when you were a kid living on a ranch?"

She looked at him. "Earl's been talking?"

"Earl knows darn near everything. Like the sheriff. I'm fairly certain he doesn't share things that are personal. Is it some kind of secret that you lived on a ranch?"

She shook her head but felt the memories jar her again, just as she thought she'd managed to put them away once more. "I just don't remember very much of it. I was seven when we moved away, so all I have left are snatches. Why?"

"I just wondered how many cold mornings you stood at the end of your road waiting for the bus. Do you remember those?"

"One or two," she admitted. "It was just me, of course,

but when it got really cold my dad would drive me to the stop and we'd wait together. Once the snow was so deep he couldn't drive me, so he forged ahead of me so I could walk." She smiled faintly, enjoying the good memory of her father. "I remember how the snow was practically up to his waist. Behind him I was walking through a tunnel."

Tim smiled. "We don't often get snow that deep right here. It tends to fall farther east because of the mountains."

She nodded, not really caring. Her only agenda was to get this house out of her hair and go home. Then she remembered Matthew. "He's taking a while with his homework. I thought he said it was just a little bit."

"Compared to what he usually has, it probably is. But he knows I'm going to check it, and he doesn't want to be sent back to fix his mistakes."

That drew another smile from her. "He's a cute kid." And he was. He could have been included in a Norman Rockwell painting.

"I think so. Of course." He looked toward the windows, as it sounded as if someone had thrown sand against them. "Ice pellets. It's begun. I need to go pull the curtains to keep this place warmer."

He closed the ones in the living room first, a deep burgundy that complimented the dark blues in the furniture and was picked up in the area rug centered on the floor. She sat by herself with the TV weather running at a quiet volume, the forecaster clearly happy to have something interesting to report.

The journey that had brought her here was certainly an odd one. She'd never expected, nor had she ever intended, to see this town or this county again. Not because anything so bad had happened to her, but because of the aftermath of what had happened to her family.

All she remembered of that time was having to move, leaving most things behind, but also leaving her friends behind. She remembered having friends back then. Not the kind of reserved friendships that came later in her life, but she'd known other people, other kids. Whisk—they were gone.

Changing schools, changing lives and listening to her father's endless bitterness. He'd turned some of that bitterness on this town and county, on the people he had known here, people he was sure were making fun of him or looking down on him.

After that move, and several others that followed, Vanessa had begun to feel like a visitor in her own life, ready to move on at a moment's notice.

But she didn't want to think about that now. Anyway, she'd been round and round about it all for years before she decided to put it away. The past couldn't be changed, and concentrating on it seemed like a waste of time.

So coming back here? That seemed like a step backward, a step in a direction she didn't want to go. Being here would resolve nothing, but it had sure stirred up a lot of unpleasant feelings and memories.

Whatever had Bob Higgins been thinking? Once upon a time she'd called him "Uncle Bob" and played with his children in that very house. Then her father had told her endlessly and repeatedly what an awful man Uncle Bob was, how he'd stolen everything from her family. She'd learned to hate him.

Now that house. It didn't make sense, and she

guessed she would never understand. She just had to find a way to dump it as quickly as possible. Get back to her normal life.

All of a sudden, Matthew came bouncing into the room. "All done! Daddy says it's okay so I can come talk to you."

She shook herself out of her reverie and summoned a smile. "You were going to show me your book."

"Later," he said decisively. "Daddy says you work with dinosaur bones. Are they really big?"

She liked his enthusiasm. "Some are huge. As long as this room. The ones I like best are the small ones, though."

"Why?" He scooted onto the other end of the couch.

Why? How to explain that to him. "Everyone loves the big bones," she said slowly. "And they're easier to find most of the time. But the little ones are like a secret."

That made his eyes shine. "Do you find out the secret?"

"Sometimes. Has anyone ever showed you a picture of the bones in your foot?"

He shook his head.

"Well, there are lots of tiny bones in your foot. Your foot wouldn't move very well without them. But someone looking at them if they were scattered around might put them together and finally figure out how your foot works."

He nodded, looking very intent. "So it's like a puzzle?"

"Exactly. Sometimes I make mistakes and put pieces from different puzzles together, and I have to figure out what's wrong. But when I find enough of the pieces of the same foot puzzle, I know how the dinosaur's foot worked."

"Do you do that all the time?"

"Once in a while."

"I'd like the small pieces, too," he decided. "More fun. But the big pieces?"

"More exciting for everyone," she agreed. "Youngsters like you are always coming to the museum to see the big dinosaurs we've managed to put together. It can be wild to stand on the floor and look up, up, up to see the head of the dinosaur. It makes me feel very small and very glad there aren't any more dinosaurs around."

He clapped his hands with delight. "I wanna do that sometime."

"I'm sure you can," Tim remarked, entering the room. "We'll take a trip and do that."

"Goody!" Matthew was satisfied. "Now can I show you my book?"

"Of course," Vanessa answered.

Matthew skipped from the room, and Tim said, "If he's imposing, let me know."

"He's not." She had to smile. "His excitement is refreshing. Too bad it's winter. There's an escarpment about a hundred miles from here where they've been making some incredible finds. Closed until spring, of course."

"I feel almost ashamed for not knowing about that dig."

She laughed, warming to him. "It's not making the news like the weather is. Most paleontologists work in obscurity unless something really big or new is discovered, and even then it rarely catches the eye of the mainstream media. You'd need to keep up with journals."

"Well, I don't have a lot of time for that, between work and child. Does a dinosaur fascination last long?"

She blinked, surprised. "In what way?"

"I mean, do kids stay interested long enough that summer can get here and I can take him to the dig?"

She laughed, shrugging. "Some kids stay fascinated for years. Others are in and out of it in a short time. The dig won't necessarily be all that interesting for him at his age, though. They might have a few things laid out on a table, but unless they're working on pulling a big piece out of the ground, it might seem dull to him." She hesitated, then said, "Listen, if it's okay with you, I can send him some materials from the museum. One of them is a wooden puzzle, where you have to put the pieces of bone together and made a 3-D model. It's really popular."

"Thank you." His smile grew wide. "I'm sure he'd love that."

"Consider it done."

How easy it was to talk about her work. But it had always been an easy topic for her. Working in a museum suited her in more ways than one. It certainly helped keep her largely by herself. Yes, she had a few girlfriends, but it wasn't the kind of closeness that would cause her to grieve if she had to move on.

Casual relationships. That was all she had, and she was content that way. Sometimes she wondered if she were just an oddity, or if she were broken in some way.

But at nearly thirty, it hardly seemed to matter. Not when she was content with her life.

Until that damn house.

Matthew bounced back in with his library book. Tim was curious to see what he'd chosen, so he sat on the far end of the sofa from Vanessa and let the boy sit between them.

It turned out to be a book of jokes, some of them well beyond the youngster's comprehension, but he seemed fascinated by all the knock-knock jokes. Tim could have groaned. He knew Matthew's memory for things that interested him, and he suspected he was going to be treated to knock-knock jokes for months. Or at least until Matthew found a new interest.

"Maybe it's time to get Harry Potter," he said.

Matthew immediately forgot his joke book. "Really?"

"Really," Tim said. He'd vastly prefer listening to summaries of the day's reading of Harry Potter than a slew of bad jokes.

"I've read Harry Potter," Vanessa volunteered. "You're going to love it."

Matthew beamed. "I think so. Ms. Macy thought I was too young." He frowned suddenly. "I don't think it's in the school library."

"Maybe not," Tim said. "It'll be in the public library, and if not, we'll go to the bookstore and get it."

"Why wouldn't it be in the public library?" Vanessa asked.

"Some people can't tell the difference between fiction and reality," he said. "Surely you remember the uproar back when about kids reading about witches and warlocks?"

"I didn't pay much attention. I was too busy reading."

He laughed. "Surely the best way to handle it."

They endured a few more bad jokes. Tim didn't mind Matthew reading them. He was, after all, reading. What he dreaded was the possibility that the boy might still find them funny and worth repeating a long time after he'd returned the book.

"Time to get the rest of dinner going," he announced. "Matthew, can you set the table?"

"The good table?"

"Of course. We have company."

Once again, Matthew dashed off to carry out his assigned task.

"You shouldn't go to any trouble for me," Vanessa protested quietly.

He shook his head a little. "This is a learning experience for Matthew. Plus, he likes being able to help. So, wanna come supervise me while I make boxed stuffing and frozen veggies? I might mess up otherwise."

The way he said it made her laugh, and she gladly followed him back into the kitchen. The rattle of ice against the windows was audible in there, and Tim felt a snaking draft.

"That cold air is the heat coming on again. It'll get warm soon. Boy, it sounds miserable out there."

"It certainly does," she agreed. "And thank you for your invitation to stay here. I'd have been miserable in the Higgins house."

"The Welling house now," he reminded her. "And you're more than welcome."

It *was* her house now, but as she watched him finish the dinner preparations, she felt an urge to share something with him, maybe so he could better understand her reactions. "Did Earl tell you what Bob Higgins did to my family? And to others around town?"

"Something about an investment scam?"

"Yeah. I don't get exactly how he did it, but he got people to give him money to invest. Periodically he'd pay out to them, especially if they had a need, but somewhere along the way he must have spent too much money to keep up the pretense that he was actually investing it. That's when he talked my father into mortgaging the ranch, promising him that his so-called investment fund would not only pay him enough to meet the mortgage payments, but would give him extra. Bob was my dad's lifelong friend. I don't think it ever entered his head that Bob was conning him."

"God, that's awful. I don't understand people who steal from others, especially when there's a trusting relationship involved."

"I don't get it, either." And it was a primary reason she found it so hard to trust. "It was especially hard on my father. He'd lost everything, we moved away and gradually he became an alcoholic. We moved again several times when he lost jobs and then…well, the alcohol killed him."

"My God! I'm so sorry, Vanessa." He'd stopped mixing the stuffing, and the vegetables were still waiting beside a microwave container. After a moment, he visibly caught himself and returned to his tasks. "I can't imagine how awful that had to have been for you."

"Eventually you don't feel it anymore. Anyway, I think the stress killed my mother. She was awfully young for a heart attack." She sighed, watching him move with the grace of a man in great shape doing the minor little things of mixing the stuffing, starting the microwave, putting a pat of butter on the bowl of frozen broccoli.

A man who could handle everything, she thought. Construction, fatherhood, cooking...he had a full plate, all right. Much fuller than hers, which seemed to be mostly filled with her own melancholy memories right now.

She missed her dinosaur bones. They spoke to her, too, but in ways that excited her. People didn't have that effect on her. She couldn't trust them to tell a true story, unlike the bones, which couldn't lie.

And that probably made her neurotic, she thought with an unexpected tickle of amusement as Matthew erupted into the kitchen. That boy was like a human power plant. "I think I did it right."

"I'll check in a moment," Tim answered. "Did you get yourself a glass of milk? And did you ask Vannie what she'd like to drink?"

Vanessa suspected this was a new stage for the boy. He looked a little surprised, then said, "I get to do the drinks?"

"You can carry a glass of milk into the dining room, can't you?"

That big, engaging grin. "Sure." He turned to Vanessa. "You want milk, too?"

"I'd very much like a glass of water, thank you."

She was charmed, enchanted, and so very glad not to be riding out this storm all alone at the Higgins house.

Matthew was just tall enough to reach the bottom shelf of the upper cupboard by stretching, and he pulled out two glasses. He stuck his tongue out and bit it while pouring one glass half-full of milk, clearly taking great care. The other was more easily handled at the sink.

Then, carefully, he picked up both glasses and carried them away.

"You must be very proud of Matthew," she remarked. Tim had pulled the stuffing from the microwave and replaced it with the frozen broccoli. The machine hummed quietly.

"I am," he agreed. He fluffed the stuffing with a fork, the recovered it with a glass lid and faced her, an easy posture leaning back against the sink. "I keep hoping Claire would feel the same."

"Your wife? I'm sure she would."

"Well, he's not perfect. He has his moments." He straightened. "I promised to check the table setting. Be right back."

Then she was alone in the kitchen, and alone with her own thoughts. Inevitably she wondered if there hadn't been something she could do about that house that wouldn't have involved her. Odd, when her memories of being there were so sketchy, that it should have such a strong impact on her.

Uncle Bob. Aunt Freda. She never heard what happened to Freda and the girls, other than that they'd left Bob behind when his misdeeds came to light. And Earl had said that Freda had changed the girls' last names. Like her family, they'd fled from destruction wrought by one man without a conscience.

Because he couldn't have had a conscience. He'd used every one of his friends in a horrible way. Her dad had just suffered the biggest losses.

Then Tim reappeared as the microwave dinged to announce the broccoli was ready.

Time for dinner.

* * *

By the time Tim decreed bedtime for Matthew, they were able to pull back the living room curtains and see a world turned into a white whirlwind that reflected the interior light.

"Not a good night to be out," Tim remarked. "I hope everyone heeded the warnings."

Matthew, Vanessa had noticed, had grown very quiet since helping to clear the table and load the dishwasher. He hadn't spoken at all.

"Are you feeling okay?" she asked him.

"He's feeling just fine," Tim said drily. "He's hoping I didn't notice that he failed to go upstairs when I said it was bedtime."

"There's no school tomorrow!" Matthew protested.

"Maybe, maybe not. We don't know for sure yet. Either way, it's bedtime for buckaroos, and yes, you can read."

Matthew tried slumping his shoulders and dragging his feet, but when that didn't get a response, he perked up and ran up the stairs.

Tim just shook his head and smiled. "There's some decent coffee in the pot if you want some. Sorry I can't offer dessert."

"I'm not used to it. It was a great dinner, though."

"Thanks. Just the basics. Anyway, I need to go up and tuck him in, make sure he doesn't skip important things like brushing his teeth. Make yourself at home."

She did just that, curling up sock-footed on the end of the couch with a scientific journal she'd pulled out of her carry-on bag.

The house had central heating, so it must have been

her imagination that it was getting colder. The coffee she'd brought in here with her helped only a little.

So she tried to bury herself in the most recent paleobiology publication. She didn't have an advanced degree, but she possessed an unquenchable curiosity about vertebrates of the past. She'd lucked into a great career field, because one of her professors in a class she'd taken just to round out her core requirements had noticed something about her and encouraged her.

She'd be forever grateful to him for that gift. And with time, she'd grown knowledgeable enough that her lack of advanced education had mattered less and less, although she picked up a course from time to time.

Tonight, though, concentrating on a morphology study didn't hold her attention. Well, of course not. She'd been going through quite an emotional earthquake since Earl Carter had called her with the news.

Lowering her head, she tried to force herself to pay attention, but the words on the page just seemed to swim in front of her. Maybe she should try reading it on her laptop, where she could magnify the print.

But there was something she'd always loved about holding a journal, the way it felt, the way it smelled, the brand-new unread pages. She viewed each one with a fresh excitement that she didn't at all feel when she read online.

So she kept trying, wondering how long it took to put a little boy to bed—and wondering why she should care. She was in a cozy place with nothing to worry her, at least until sometime tomorrow.

Between one breath and the next, she drifted off with the journal in her hand and her head on the overstuffed arm of the sofa.

* * *

Tim had one of those revelations that only a parent could have. When he helped Matthew get into his pajamas, he discovered the boy was wearing four pairs of briefs.

"What's this?" he asked, genuinely curious. "Why so many?"

"You told me to put on new ones every day."

Apparently, he'd left out an important part of the instructions, Tim thought as laughter rose in him. He quelled it, funny though this was, because another thought occurred to him: the boy couldn't have been bathing. He wouldn't have worn all those underpants if they were wet.

"Okay," he said slowly. "And how do you handle your socks?"

"New ones every day. I was going to tell you my shoes are getting tight, too."

Tim could easily imagine that they were, even though they were almost new. "So how many socks do you have on each foot?"

"Four."

"What started all this?" he asked, genuinely curious.

"When you were doing the laundry and said I hadn't worn enough underpants or socks for a week. Fresh ones every day."

Tim remembered that conversation clearly. Oh, man. "I left out part of the instructions, kiddo. The part about taking off the dirty ones before you put on fresh ones. Come on, let's get rid of all these in the hamper and put you in the shower."

Tim wondered if he'd ever learn how literal a child

could be. Probably not. He'd keep making these simple mistakes until Matthew grew up enough to fill in the blanks.

With his son showered, dried and in fresh pajamas, Tim scooped him up and carried him to bed. God, it felt so good to have this boy in his arms. He smelled sweet and just so right. Not much more of this, though. One way or another, Matthew was going to get too big, and from what he'd seen of slightly older kids, he'd be lucky to snag a hug.

But for now he took pleasure in the moment and just wished Claire could share it, too.

Sometimes he felt his wife around, as if she peeked in on them, as if her love still existed. Maybe it did. And maybe, like an angel, she kept watch over Matthew. He certainly hoped so.

Though it had been six years since Claire's unexpected passing, he still missed her. Missed all the little things they had shared, which in retrospect seemed a whole lot more important than the big things.

Glances over breakfast that seemed to warm the air. Shared looks of understanding that needed no words. Being able to reach out and just hold her hand. Those little things had turned into a huge gap in his life.

He wanted no replacement for Claire. He didn't think it was possible, and he wasn't looking. Most especially he didn't want to upset Matthew's life. His son seemed to have adapted quite well to the fact that he didn't have a mother, unlike his friends.

Whenever someone pressed Tim on the subject—and yes, he knew they did out of some kind of concern—he simply said that was for later. After Matthew was grown. Safely down the road and something he didn't need to think about now. Not when he had his son to concern him, and not when he was still aching with loss.

He was learning that you never stopped grieving. It just softened with time. Or became like a comfortable old friend, always there, never gone. At least it didn't cripple him the way it once had. He could pause, absorb and acknowledge the pain, then keep going.

Matthew made that essential.

Downstairs, he found Vanessa curled up on the couch and sound asleep. He thought about moving her to her room then decided against disturbing her. If she woke up on her own, she could go to her room then. In the meantime, she looked comfortable, and it wouldn't be the first time that sofa had been a bed.

Out in the kitchen, he opened his laptop and logged in while he brewed fresh coffee. He had more jobs than the Higgins house. There were a couple of remodel and repair jobs he'd promised to email estimates on by Saturday, and he needed to finish them.

He paused a moment, thinking of the woman sleeping in his living room. What a cutie, he decided. A lovely woman, and she'd handled Matthew's sometimes overwhelming energy well.

Then he returned to work. Two things in his life, mainly. His son and his work. Everything else paled beside them.

Chapter Three

Vanessa awoke in the dark. All the lights in the room were off, and in a faint spill of light coming from elsewhere, she needed a couple of seconds to orient herself. Tim Dawson's house. Conard County. *Oh, God.*

She sat up, rotating her shoulders and neck to ease the stiffness, and put her slightly crumpled journal to one side. How rude of her. The man had given her shelter, served her a fine meal, and she'd responded by falling asleep on his sofa while he put his son to bed?

Well, maybe he wasn't terribly offended. She guessed she'd have to wait until morning to find out. She could hear the blizzard now, howling outside as if it were alive. She was *so* glad she wasn't alone in that ruin of a house she'd inherited, or at the motel where she'd be stuck in one room alone, probably listening to the more regular patrons celebrate the weather with whiskey.

In fact, though she didn't drink often, a whiskey didn't sound too bad to her, either.

She rose, grateful she'd changed into comfy fleece earlier, and stretched every muscle in her body. There was nothing quite like a good stretch. Feeling better, she headed toward the light, which was coming from the kitchen, and was surprised to see Tim at the kitchen table, computer in front of him and stacks of paper surrounding him.

He looked up at once and smiled. "Good nap?"

"I was so out of it," she admitted. "I'm sorry I fell asleep on you."

"I don't remember inviting you here to be entertaining. You obviously needed the sleep."

"And I really could use some water. My mouth feels so parched. Oh, God," she added as the thought struck her, "was I snoring?"

"If you were, I didn't notice. Do you want the chilled bottled water? Or would you rather have something else? I finished the coffee, but I have soft drinks—all the diet variety, I'm afraid—or I could make hot chocolate."

"Right now just water would be great." Moving by instinct, she found the glasses in the upper cupboard beside the sink. "You want any?"

"I'm fine."

She chose to get water from the tap and drained a whole glass before she left the sink, then filled it again halfway and ventured to join him at the table. "Working?"

"Yup. Almost done."

"Don't let me disturb you."

Sipping her water, she closed her eyes, listening to

the sounds of the storm outside, and the sounds the house made in response. A gust of wind could cause the slight creaking from somewhere upstairs. If snow was falling, it was mixed with ice that rattled against the window glass. Without even looking she was grateful not to be out in it.

Or, frankly, by herself.

For some reason, being in this town had made her feel isolated. Maybe because she'd left behind the friendly faces of her coworkers and her immediate neighbors in her apartment building.

Maybe because since she'd arrived, she'd met three strangers and knew very little about any of them. Matthew probably couldn't be included in that, though. There was little doubt as to what he thought about anything.

But Earl, even though she'd talked to him a number of times on the phone, was still a stranger. And for all she was sharing Tim's house tonight, she knew very little about him except he was a contractor, he had a son and he'd lost his wife.

Just an outline. But what did he know about her? That she worked with dinosaur bones in a museum, that her family had lost everything to Bob Higgins and that she didn't want this house that had fallen into her lap.

He probably wondered why that was. Not everyone would look at a free house as a problem, even if it did need work.

She had to admit she wasn't sure herself why she was reacting so strongly. Yeah, the man had cost her family everything and turned them into wanderers. Yes, her father had drunk himself to death, but that had been his choice, not Bob's. She'd suffered because of what had happened nearly twenty years ago, but this seemed to go beyond bad memories.

Maybe it had bored a hole in her soul, somehow.

With a snap that startled her eyes open, she heard Tim close his computer case. "Done," he said. "For now, anyway. When the numbers start to look like fish swimming through a tank, it's usually a good time to stop."

She liked his ready sense of humor. She envied that it seemed to come so easily to him. She wasn't a very humorous person herself. In fact, if asked, she'd probably classify herself as...too reserved, she decided finally. Not sour, but reserved.

"So, about your house," he said. "It's structurally sound. A couple of roof rafters could use replacing because they got wet at some point, but there's no dampness up there now. You could probably let those skate."

She nodded, feeling unready to discuss this, but knowing she couldn't evade it indefinitely. After all, she'd come back to take care of it, and an inheritance from Bob that she hadn't turned down was the last of his savings. She figured since he'd dumped his white elephant on her, she needed the money to fix it up and pay the taxes. She just hoped it was enough. Lowly museum assistants didn't make huge salaries.

"To make the house interesting to a buyer, there are some basic things we need to do. Caulking. The weatherizing in the windows and doors is cracked, unattended for too long. The attic fan is dead. The floors sag and are weak in a few places." He stopped. "I don't want to overwhelm you. The question is, do you want to pull it together just enough to hopefully attract someone by marketing it as a major fixer-upper? That'll cost you a pretty penny in terms of what you can make off it, and frankly, with the amount of cosmetics it needs, that might not even work. You saw the paint sagging on the wall. I don't like that."

"It's ugly," she agreed.

"It's more than ugly. It might be lead based."

Her heart lurched. "I thought that was illegal!"

"It is now. But it was only in 1978 that it was banned in housing. Now how many walls do you think got painted over with latex or oil-based paints and never stripped?"

Her mind was dancing around as if she had hot coals inside it. She didn't want to hear this. Want to or not, she was stuck with it. "We should knock it down and clear the lot."

"Maybe. I'm going to have an inspector check the place out first." He popped open his computer. "I reckon if there's lead, knocking it down and clearing out the remains will cost as much as a basic fixup and getting rid of as much lead paint as we might find. And—here's the important thing—unless you can sell that empty lot, you'll still owe taxes as if the house was on it."

She was flummoxed. "Really? *Really?*"

"Best and highest use."

That did it. Vanessa put her head in her hands and muttered, "I want my dinosaur bones."

"Earl mentioned that you wanted to donate the house, but ask yourself if it would be ethical to give it to a church or preschool before we deal with any health threats."

Her head snapped up. "Of course not!"

He smiled. "Good."

Then his question struck her. "You certainly didn't imagine that I'd pass that lead paint along, especially to children."

"In this world," he said slowly, "you never know. I've had people come to me who wanted to cover a multitude of sins with fresh paint or linoleum."

"So Bob Higgins wasn't the only con artist around here."

"I wish I could say he was." He rose and stretched his arms, making her acutely aware of his flat belly. "Let's go back to your bedroom. No, I'm not sending you to bed, but I want to be sure you know where everything is and feel free to use it."

This time, having escaped her self-absorption, she knew instantly that this room had once been the master bedroom. Those forget-me-nots and the colors were his wife's choices, she had realized earlier, but now they took on meaning that almost made her squirm.

"Private shower, too," he remarked, pointing to a closed door.

She wanted to ask outright but caught herself. No point in prodding this man's wounds. She ought to understand that herself. "Where do you sleep?"

"Upstairs, just down the hall from Matthew. He used to have nightmares and be scared there was something under his bed."

She suspected that was only part of the reason, but it was good enough. "I hope he's outgrown that."

"Mostly. It still happens occasionally. So, when we can get out into the world, do you want to go over your house with me? I can make a list of the absolute essentials, but I still need your input."

She nodded slowly. "I'm still trying to figure out why I hate that house. I know why I didn't want to come back to this town. My dad spent his last years vilifying this place. But the house? I vaguely remember having fun there as a child."

He tilted his head to one side. "Why was your dad so down on the town? They didn't rip him off."

"I think he believed people around here thought he was an absolute fool. He felt they were judging him."

He nodded slowly. "Higgins was your dad's friend, right?"

"Lifelong."

"Well, I reckon I'd get a bit paranoid, too, if my best friend stole everything from me and my family. I'd feel like an idiot for having trusted him, I'd feel wounded beyond words and, yeah, maybe I'd feel like I was in the public stocks, when in truth a lot of people were probably thinking, *there but for the grace of God.*"

She sighed. "You might be right. I just know what my dad believed. Anyway, I never wanted to come back here, and Earl probably told you how badly I wanted to get out from under that house."

He pursed one side of his mouth, then said, "Well, judging by what Higgins did, you could always just deed it over to someone else. Just quitclaim it to some wealthy guy half a continent away. Won't he get a shock?"

She laughed. She couldn't help it—the idea was so funny. "That wouldn't be a nice thing to do."

"It wasn't nice that Higgins bombed you this way, either."

She looked away suddenly, realizing that he might have just touched on the core of her problem with this whole mess. Not the past at all, but the present. A house she hadn't wanted, a headache, an expense. Like Bob Higgins was reaching out from the grave for one last swipe. "You think he was bombing me?" Her voice had tightened, and tension arose within her again. Mainly because Tim seemed to be confirming her own suspicions, suspicions she'd been trying to ignore.

"Truthfully? I don't know." He led her down the short hall back to the kitchen. There he asked her if she wanted some cocoa or warm milk. She opted for the cocoa. "Thank you."

"I don't know about you," he remarked, "but when it's howling and cold like that outside, I feel an urge to get cozy inside. It's not like that cold out there is reaching me. Some atavistic response, I guess."

Interesting choice of words from a guy who made his living as a building contractor. For the first time, it crossed her mind that she might have become a bit of a snob over the years. An intellectual snob. Why wouldn't the man be smart and have a great command of the language? Because he worked with his hands? That didn't mean he didn't have a brain.

Man, this whole trip was shaking her up in so many ways. Facing a childhood she couldn't remember, facing once again the years of her dad's deterioration, facing an anger that had been planted in her by chaos and one man's bitterness.

She wasn't ready for any of this, yet here it was. And she sure as hell didn't want to deal with it right now. "If you owned the house," she said slowly, "what would you want to do with it?"

"Now that's an interesting question." He made the

cocoa from packets and only needed to add boiling water. Soon he was sitting at the kitchen table with her again.

She waited, watching him slowly stir his mug with a spoon as he thought about it. He wasn't going to treat the question lightly.

"The house-flipping business isn't exactly booming around here," he remarked. "Real estate sales are sluggish. Not dead, but not fast, either."

Oh, great, she thought. She'd probably be stuck with that damn house forever.

"Anyway, if I were going to own two houses here, I'd fix up the Higgins place, stem to stern, and sell this house."

His answer truly surprised her. "But why? This is a beautiful house!"

"Also a size that would be easier to sell," he said with a shrug. "Already beautifully decorated. By my wife."

She bit her lip, feeling uncomfortable. She usually kept a safe distance from others, riding the surface of emotions without getting caught in the deep waves. But Tim's simple statement pierced her armor a bit, and she felt sorrow for him. "That must be...difficult for you."

"Not exactly the word I'd use. It does remind me of her and that I miss her. It may be time for me to move on. As for Matthew, he doesn't remember her at all. She's photos in an album. Moving around the corner would probably be an exciting adventure for him."

"But why take on a house you couldn't sell?" she pressed.

"Because I wouldn't want to sell it. Fixing it up bit

by bit would probably take most of the rest of my life. A major project."

That sounded so darn lonely to her. Here he was living in a beautiful house he probably felt he couldn't change, a kind of memorial. Changing it would be like erasing his late wife. A new house…a clean slate. And he'd be busy with it.

For the first time, she considered that the Higgins house wasn't just a pain for her. Something she had never wanted, something she didn't want to deal with. Maybe she needed an attitude adjustment. Tim obviously thought the house had potential and promise. Maybe she should try a different perspective, if she could manage it. However this fell out, she wasn't going to be here long, and she should stop resenting it and just deal with it. Maybe even enjoy it a bit. Somehow.

"What happened to your wife?" she asked, hoping she wasn't being intrusive. Somewhere in the fog of the upheaval that had been dominating her mind, she had the feeling he had already told her. Had he? If so, forgetting about something so important to him should embarrass her.

"Pulmonary embolism," he answered matter-of-factly. Maybe he hadn't told her before. "Blood clot in the lung. They were never able to pin down the cause, but I guess that doesn't matter. What matters is that it was fast for her."

"That's so sad."

He nodded. "Goes without saying. So, yeah, I'd take that house and make it over, and when I got done it would be a jewel. And I'd enjoy every minute of making it into one."

"I could quitclaim it to you," she remarked.

He laughed. "I wouldn't feel right about that. Don't even consider it. I'm sure we can get you something out of that property. And whatever we get would be rightfully yours, if you ask me."

The storm continued to rage throughout the night. Tim didn't sleep well, but he seldom did when the weather turned bad. Claire had called him the night watchman, laughing as she did so, but bad weather made him restless. He wasn't expecting anything terrible tomorrow, except a lot of shoveling. But he still got restless.

After Vanessa went to bed, he walked in socks around the house, up the stairs and back down again. He'd warned her he might pace, so she wouldn't worry if she heard anything, but he tried to keep his step light and silent anyway.

Moving away from this house? He hadn't been kidding when he told Vanessa it might be time for him to move on. There were a lot of ways he could do that, though. The first one was simple: redecorate.

The problem with that was equally simple. Claire's taste and identity were stamped all over this house. It was odd how easy it was for him to remember each new find of hers and how excited she had been about them. The way the structure of this house had taken on a whole personality because of her. Simply wiping away the beauty she'd created here felt like a betrayal of sorts. As if he were erasing her from his life.

She could never be erased.

So moving on might literally require moving. He

couldn't, not with his own two hands, remove her from this house. So, yeah, if he owned the Higgins place, he'd let someone else make the changes here as they wanted and he'd start a whole new project.

But he didn't own the Higgins house, and he hoped Vanessa had just been joking about turning it over to him. He didn't want that, would never want that. He hoped he'd made that clear enough.

Then his thoughts turned to Vanessa. Quite a pretty young woman, especially those mossy-green eyes of hers. He didn't think he'd ever seen quite that color before. It reminded him of a creek bank in the summertime shade. Peaceful.

But he felt little peace in her. She had relaxed when talking about her work, but then he felt invisible walls rising, putting space between her and everything else. It wasn't just the reserve one might feel with a stranger. It felt to him like something much more, something much deeper.

So maybe he ought to stop thinking about how pretty she was, or the way her sweater earlier in the day had cuddled her breasts and revealed a surprisingly tiny waist.

She had the kind of figure a man could dream about, from what he could guess through her clothes, even the loose fleece she had put on after arriving here.

Another kind of complication he didn't need in his life. He had a son to think about and was scrupulous in his behavior as a result. If he went out on a date, which was rare, he was always home at an early hour. Setting an example, he hoped. Making Matthew feel secure, he hoped.

Not that Matthew seemed to have any major insecurities. If he did, he hid them well for a child his age.

But being a solo parent had made him acutely aware of his responsibilities. He didn't have a backup crew to step in and pick up any slack or correct any of his mistakes. Matthew wasn't by any measure a difficult child, and his heart seemed to be in the right place. But Tim was acutely aware that if he made mistakes they might affect the boy for life.

The school counselor had told him to relax a bit. There was no evidence he was doing anything wrong. But he could never quite believe it. He was flying on a wing and a prayer.

The wind blew another blast of ice at the windows. As cold as it was, the snow shouldn't be icy. At least that's what he thought, but he could be wrong. He could be wrong about so many things.

Finally pulling out his laptop, he looked up digs for dinosaur fossils in Wyoming. If Matthew was still interested come early summer, they ought to take that trip that Vanessa had suggested. There was one museum, a little on the expensive side, that would take the two of them out to participate in a dig. For his own part, he was more interested in something less commercial.

He was sure he could find an opportunity, especially with Vanessa's help. He had no trouble imagining Matthew's excitement, even if all they did was watch from the sidelines or see some bones emerging from the ground.

Then he remembered Vanessa putting her head in her hands and saying she wanted her bones back. It had been cute, and funny, and so terribly truthful all at once.

Bones would certainly be more peaceful. But life seldom left anyone alone.

He closed his computer after checking the weather report, then shut his eyes for a few minutes, just listening. The storm wasn't easing yet. Time to take another swing by Matthew's room, make sure he was still sleeping.

As for himself, he really ought to try to get some shut-eye. Thing was, he knew all he'd do was try. All his life, storms at night had made him restless. He could never explain why.

In her own room, the former master bedroom, Vanessa listened to Tim's quiet movements through the house and tried to get some sleep herself. After all that had happened today—the long drive from the airport, her viewing of a house that had somehow become part of her nightmares and her evening with Tim and Matthew— she ought to be ready to crash.

Instead she remained wakeful, listening to a restless man walk the hours of the night. She wondered if it was really that storms made him edgy or if it had other roots. But why should she wonder? If he'd been dealing with it for a long time, he probably understood it better than she ever could with a few guesses.

Though the bed was comfortable and the room cozy, she couldn't help wishing she were home in her own bed, facing another day in the bowels of the museum sorting through bones, making sure they were properly identified and preserved. So much that came out of fossil beds had been protected by nature for ages, but once exposed, all the elements of decay could resume their work. Especially since they had found that in many dinosaur bones the marrow still contained living tissue. Which had, amusingly enough, explained the slightly unpleasant smell paleontologists had been associating with those bones for a long time.

But she was comfortable in that environment, sure in her knowledge, excited by possibilities, and enjoying the scientific conversation and discussion. Definitely in her element.

Now she had been yanked away, however briefly, to face an environment she didn't know how to handle as well, leaving her comfort zone so far behind she almost felt like she was in free fall. What was going to happen from all of this? Would she be able to deal with those old demons, many of which traced directly back to her father, some of which were due to being uprooted so many times?

Did she *have* to deal with anything?

Oddly, she realized she was envying Matthew. Stable home, great father, an unshadowed childhood. Which assumed a lot, she admitted to herself. She didn't really know him yet—or Tim, for that matter.

But Tim was thinking he might move on. Her idea of moving on wasn't a good one. She hoped that it wouldn't adversely affect Matthew.

Then, with the quiet footsteps becoming a background to the storm, she drifted into dreams.

Matthew's piping voice awoke her in the morning. Half dozing, she listened to Tim trying to make him speak more quietly, but that amount of energy couldn't be easily contained.

It was still dark outside, and for some reason that made her think of Christmases when she was really young and couldn't wait for her parents to come tell her that Santa had been there.

Those days had been much better, much happier, and to be fair, until the mess with Higgins had blown up, she'd had a happy childhood. Probably much like Matthew's, except Matthew didn't have a mother.

She wondered how much that saddened him, or if he just felt it was the normal way of things. According to Tim, he couldn't remember her at all. But other kids had mothers. Maybe that had an impact. To judge by the sound of Matthew's voice right now, however, the boy was perfectly happy to be facing a snow day.

The sounds made her smile.

A little later, after a nice warm shower, she dressed in her warmest fleece and socks, and made her way to the happy sounds in the kitchen. Just as she opened the bedroom door, she heard Tim say, "She's not here yet. Hold your horses. You're not going to starve before I find out if she wants any."

Her smile grew wider as she walked down the polished hall, around the dining room into the kitchen. Before she had a chance to say good morning, Matthew was hopping up in front of her.

"You want pancakes, don't you? With *real* maple syrup?"

"Let the lady open her eyes," Tim scolded mildly.

"I'd love pancakes," she assured Matthew, then took Tim's gesture to sit at the kitchen table.

"With *real* maple syrup," Matthew reminded her.

"I haven't had any real maple syrup in years." She smiled her thanks as Tim put coffee in front of her.

"It's a treat," Matthew informed her. "Daddy says it's expensive, so we only have it once in a while."

"Like once a year," Tim interjected. "You want anything in your coffee?"

"Black is great," she answered.

"Settle, son," Tim said to the boy, "or I won't dare let you help with the pancakes."

Matthew immediately embarked on a valiant effort to contain his excitement. Vanessa decided pancakes weren't a regular item in this household. Still, even though he grew quiet, the boy's energy was palpable.

He climbed on a step stool beside the counter, while Tim measured the mix and milk into a large bowl, and listened intently as Tim told him they didn't want to mix it too much. Beside them was an electric griddle, and Tim showed how to test when it was ready by flicking a little water on it.

"See the droplets dance? That says the griddle is really hot and ready. Now remember, pancakes don't take long. You're going to start with a small one, okay?"

Vanessa enjoyed the entire show, start to finish. Matthew managed to make himself a stack of small pancakes, and Tim brought a plate of larger ones to the table. Vanessa offered to set the table, but Tim rightly pointed out she didn't know her way around the kitchen and it would only take Matthew a moment. He proved it. Almost instantly she had a plate, fork and knife in front of her. A butter dish was added, and soon they were all eating.

Vanessa savored the maple syrup and commented on it.

"I told you it was good," Matthew said immediately.

"Special treat," she agreed. "A very special one."

Tim spoke. "Hardly worth making pancakes without it."

Matthew giggled. "You make them with blueberry jam, and sometimes with cinnamon and sugar."

"And not very often."

Matthew screwed up his face. "I know. Not healthy."

Tim chuckled. "Anyway, Vanessa, we're going to be shoveling snow as soon as the storm lets up some more, and Matthew wants to make a snowman. Care to join us?"

"That sounds like fun." She meant it, and realized that her discomfort with coming back to this town was rapidly evaporating. She didn't feel as if she were wearing the mark of Cain, and now that she was here, she thought how silly her concerns had been. Why should anyone care what had happened over twenty years ago? And even if they did, she'd been a child like Matthew back then, not responsible for any of it.

Of course, there was still the house, but as she got her feet under her, she was beginning to think she'd be able to handle that. She'd face it and deal. She could do that.

A smile remained on her face as she helped load dishes into the dishwasher after Matthew and Tim emptied the previous load. While they put them away, she watched so she could learn. If she was invited to stay over again tonight, she wanted to be able to help more.

It was still snowing rather heavily, a fact that Vanessa had utterly missed because all the curtains were drawn against the cold. But when Tim peeled back the curtain over the sink, she saw white flakes whirling everywhere.

"This is so cool!" Matthew pronounced.

"You think so?" Tim answered. "Wait till I hand you that shovel." He dropped the curtain and eyed Vanessa. "You may not remember, but heavy snow didn't used to be common. Now we're seeing more of it. Back when, most of the snow dropped before the storm crossed the mountains, and then dropped the rest farther east. These days we're getting snowed in almost as much as anybody else."

"That's cool," Matthew insisted. "Maybe no school again tomorrow."

"Don't count on it, kiddo. These roads will be clean before the day is over."

Not even that dampened Matthew, however. He skated off to the living room, announcing he was going to pick a DVD to watch.

"The creeks and ponds will be full this spring," Tim said as he joined her at the table with some coffee for himself. She declined his offer of more. "Happy ranchers. Water can often be a problem around here. As for your house..." He shook his head. "A lot of shoveling and plowing is going to have to happen before we can get over there."

"I'm not exactly on the edge of my seat," she admitted.

"What is it about that house?" he asked. "It's just a building, but it seems to mean a whole lot more to you."

She looked down, running her fingertip slowly across the tabletop as if she were doodling invisibly. "It's hard to explain," she admitted. "It's more feelings that any specific thing. Mixed feelings."

"I'm interested," he said.

She could have felt pushed. This was some pretty

personal territory. But for some reason, she felt the question was friendly, not prying.

She hesitated for another few seconds, seeking words that wouldn't sound totally crazy. "I had a lot of fun there when I was little. Bob had two kids, just a little older than me, and we'd go over to visit the family on weekends. The girls and I played a lot, and Bob often had some little gift for me. My parents and Bob and his wife seemed to be really good friends. I always looked forward to those visits."

"I see. But then it changed."

"Radically. At first I didn't even grasp that something bad was going on. We stopped going over there, but I knew my dad still went. Then there were angry phone calls. Any time I asked when we were going over there again, I was told that they weren't our friends anymore. I didn't get it. I didn't even really get it when we moved across the country, except that I lost everything and everyone I knew except my parents. It was years before I began to find out what had happened."

"And when you did, you knew where to focus a whole lot of confusion and hurt."

"Oh, yeah," she said. "Oh, yeah." She sighed. "I know it was long ago, but it changed me, changed my life. Things were never the same again. Never. I remember that we'd been a happy family up until then. Afterward…no happiness left."

"I'm really sorry. That's a sad story. And all because of one man's greed."

"My dad trusted him," she said, finally raising her gaze, but not to look at Tim. Instead she looked toward the sink, finding it easier than seeing an expression on another's face. After all these years. All these years and those old pains could rise up and strike her in the face. Shouldn't she have outgrown all that by now?

She certainly thought she had, but this trip, this entire series of events, was teaching her that it wasn't true, that all she'd done was bury things that, zombie-like, could rise up with the right stimulus.

Tim spoke. "Your dad's trust being abused that way...that's the hard part to swallow, I'd think."

She nodded slightly, unsure if she agreed.

"For me, at least," he continued, "I think I could deal with the loss of everything I own better than I could deal with someone abusing my trust and friendship so egregiously. But it's never happened to me, so I don't know what I'm talking about."

"You may be right," she said after a few seconds. "Like I said, it's all mixed up. My dad never recovered, whether it was from being treated that way by a friend, or from losing everything he and his family had worked for, or from both. And I got it all secondhand. All I know is he drank himself to death over the next fifteen years, we had to keep moving because he'd lose his job and have to find another, and every move stressed my mother and required *her* to find a new job. She didn't survive him for very long."

He shook his head, frowning sadly. "That's bad. I'm not surprised you don't want that house. Didn't want any reminders like that."

"I can't imagine what Higgins was thinking," she admitted, her voice taking on an edge. "My dear old uncle Bob, as I used to call him. Destroyed my family then dumps this on me? Earl keeps trying to make it sound like Bob regretted what he'd done and wanted to make up for it. I don't think he was capable of any such thing, Tim."

"Maybe not." He paused. "Probably not. A guy who could do what he did—if he didn't have a conscience back then, I doubt he grew one in prison."

"Me, too. You know, part of what made it so hard on my dad, I think, was that his trust for Bob's financial management abilities helped draw in other people. I don't think he felt ashamed just because he got robbed, but because he unwittingly helped others get robbed. I think that's the reason he always felt that he'd be judged harshly if he came back here."

"That could be." Tim paused thoughtfully. "Did he make you feel that way, too, that folks here would judge you?"

Stupid as it sounded, she admitted it. "Yes."

"Now I'm really sorry. I'm sure we have some rotten apples here—what place doesn't?—but you were only seven. How could anyone hold you responsible?"

"I know it sounds silly." She shrugged one shoulder. "It seems I have some leftover hang-ups."

"Coming back here would certainly wake them up. Want some fresh coffee or something else?"

She'd only downed half the cup he'd given her before breakfast, and she realized that the taste of maple remained on her tongue, growing a bit cloying. "Coffee, please."

He rose, emptied her cup in the sink and poured fresh for both of them before returning to sit across from her. From the living room, she could hear the noises of what sounded like a fast-paced cartoon. It wasn't a far reach to remember her own snowy mornings and weekends in the Before Days, as she thought of them. When it had been too bitterly cold to run around outside, only then had she been allowed to watch TV in the daytime.

Her spirits began to rise again, and she decided to push off the entire matter of Higgins and her family for another time. It was beginning to seem that she'd be dealing with this mess for the rest of her life. That didn't mean she couldn't have fun in between.

"Matthew is adorable," she said, pointedly changing the topic.

"I agree, of course." He smiled. "I think shoveling will slow him down a bit. Then a snowman. When was the last time you made one?"

"A snowman? When I was Matthew's age. It used to drive me crazy, though, because I could never get them to look like a drawing or photo, perfectly rounded. Mine looked kinda clunky."

"Well, we'll work on that skill today," he joked.

She grinned. "I could always find rocks for the nose and eyes, but Mom would never part with a carrot. Anyway, I was never really happy with ones I made."

"Did you have any help?"

"I was a singleton, and no one else on the ranch was interested. Too busy."

"Well, nobody's too busy today."

She decided that sounded really good.

Chapter Four

Many hands made for swift work in clearing the snow, and for the first time Vanessa helped build a snowman that looked as if it had stepped from the pages of a storybook. Matthew and Tim showed her how to smooth it out, and Tim wasn't stingy with the carrot. He even broke off some small limbs from his shrubbery to make arms.

"Want a photo of that?" he asked with a wide smile.

The shoveling and building of the snowman had kept them warm, but finally they started to chill and headed inside. Tim served up a big pot of hot chocolate along with some chicken soup.

"Not the best flavor combination," he remarked, "but I think it's going to go down well."

Vanessa admired the easy way he handled everything. He could repair things, build things, clear a side-walk, make a snowman and cook very well. A man of many talents.

A very handsome man of many talents.

But then she reminded herself not to pay attention to her unexpected attraction to him. She was just passing through, the way she had for most of her life. Senseless to invest herself in people she wouldn't know for long. As a self-protective posture, it had become part of her personality, and it worked. Even at the museum, where she would probably continue working for a great many years, she kept a certain reserve, a space between herself and her coworkers.

"So what's it like working at the museum?" Tim asked as they ate. "Lots of interesting people, I bet."

"Dinosaurs," said Matthew, almost as if he were correcting his father.

"Well, yes, dinosaurs," she agreed. "And knowledgeable people. I learn something every day." She turned to Matthew. "But I don't only work with dinosaur bones."

His eyes widened a shade. "Really? Is there other good stuff, too?"

She had to laugh. "Lots of good stuff. Bones don't have to be big to tell a story."

Matthew thought about that while he drank cocoa then looked at her while wearing a chocolate mustache. "How can bones talk?"

That was one of her favorite subjects. "They don't talk like you and I do. But they definitely have stories to tell. When I study them, I can learn when they lived and how they lived, and maybe even how they died. I can tell if they were babies, or grown-ups, and did they live alone or have families. Now, not every bone is going to give me all that information, but with time and more bones, it's like putting a puzzle together into a picture."

He nodded, evidently grasping what she was saying. "So they don't tell a story but they make a puzzle picture."

"That's one way of looking at it," she agreed. "But over time I get more than just one puzzle picture. That's when I start to get a story."

"Okay. But dinosaur bones are the best."

She and Tim laughed. "You come visit my museum sometime, and I'll show you."

"Uh-oh," said Tim just before Matthew turned to him.

"Can we, Dad? Can we?"

"Albuquerque is a bit of a drive," he answered.

Vanessa hesitated, realizing she had put him on the spot without intending to. "Sorry," she said to Tim.

His smile turned crooked. "Frankly, I was expecting this from the moment you mentioned dinosaurs. We'll see, Matthew. We couldn't go before next summer, regardless. And maybe by then you'll want to go to a truck museum."

Vanessa stifled a laugh, pressing her lips tightly together.

"I don't like trucks that much," Matthew said decisively. "Anyway, they don't have museums."

"I wouldn't be so sure of that," Tim replied. "There seem to be museums for just about anything."

But Matthew was already moving on. "Do you dig up the bones?" he asked Vanessa.

"Sometimes," she answered.

"I wanna do that."

"Maybe you'll get the chance. It's fun—for a little while, anyway. Then it gets hot, you get tired, and it takes a long, long time to get some little bone out of the ground. Longer for a big bone."

Tim spoke. "I take it you prefer working in the museum."

"Mostly. But I get into the field once in a while. When I'm there I don't do much of the digging, but I do a lot of preservation work. Some of those bones come out of the stone ready to crumble. They haven't been exposed the elements for maybe millions of years, and they start deteriorating the minute they hit the air and humidity."

"I never thought about that."

She was grateful to him for keeping the subject in a safe area—safe for her. Because tomorrow they were going to have to make their way back to the Higgins house, and she was going to have to face some very old demons. She'd rather pull bones out of limestone. "We try to preserve right at the site if we can."

Easier to talk about than that damn house. She'd been able to forget it most of the day, but now it was looming again. It seemed ridiculous to give it so much power over her. She'd survived that period of her life, after all, even though it had eventually cost her so much.

But the simple fact was that over the years she'd learned to hate it. Or fear it. She couldn't decide which. Everything about that period had gotten tangled in her mind as a child, and it seemed that growing up hadn't untwisted the knot.

Later that evening, after Matthew had gone to bed

for the night, she and Tim relaxed in the living room. She sat on one end of the dark blue couch while he sat on the other. On the coffee table was a small plate of bakery cookies.

The wind had picked up again, rattling the windows just a bit, and Tim remarked that he hoped they didn't need to shovel again tomorrow.

"When the snow gets dry enough, and the wind blows hard enough, I can shovel the same dang snow six or seven times. It's annoying. One blizzard with reruns."

She smiled at his description. "We don't see much snow in Albuquerque, although we get some. Usually light, rarely more than an inch or two. I mean, you have to spread eleven inches of snow over the whole winter, on average. We might get a powder this month, like confectioner's sugar, but the most of it will come after Christmas. I consider that a plus, I guess."

"Right now, I would, too. But I like living here, for the most part." He hesitated then said, "Thinking about the house is still bothering you, isn't it?"

"Yes," she admitted, her lips growing tight. "It's not just the reality of what happened."

"No?"

Then, on impulse, she told him something she'd never shared with anyone else. "I have nightmares about that house. Which is weird, because I always had fun when I was there. But the nightmares have come from time to time over the years."

"Nightmares how?"

"It starts off feeling normal, but then everything

changes. I'm all alone, and it gets darker. You know how the upstairs has that hallway?"

He nodded. "L-shaped with three bedrooms coming off it, and the bath."

"Exactly. Except in my dream when I climb the stairs, it straightens out and seems to go on forever. A long, long hallway lined with closed doors. The closest thing I've ever seen to it is a hotel. Anyway, I know it's Uncle Bob's house, but I'm afraid of all those doors. Afraid of what's behind them. And all I know is that I *have* to walk past all of them to the other end. I don't have a choice."

"That's creepy," he said quietly.

"It sure feels that way when I'm dreaming it. But it sounds almost absurd when I say it out loud."

"I don't think so. I can imagine it, actually. Everything distorted, so you know where you are, but it looks different, and all those closed doors that could conceal anything? Creepy. Nightmares are more about feelings than images anyway, don't you think?"

"Depends," she said after a few seconds' thought. "But mostly I agree with you. There haven't been too many horrific images in my nightmares, but there's always been plenty of fear or terror. Urgency."

He nodded and draped his arm along the back of the couch while crossing his legs loosely. He looked so relaxed that she envied him. Her entire body ought to be relaxing, too, with all that time spent shoveling and building a snowman. But instead of feeling weary, she felt herself winding up. Anxiety about tomorrow?

"I could quitclaim the house to you," she blurted. "You said you'd love to make it over, to move on."

At that she felt tension run through him, although he didn't seem to move a muscle. "No."

"No?"

"Come on, Vanessa. You deserve to get *something* out of this mess, miserable though it's making you. Secondly, I wouldn't accept it, because it feels wrong. Unethical."

"But I want to get rid of it. I told you."

He looked straight at her. "Yeah, you did. But what you really need is to deal with it."

His blunt statement deprived her of breath. He was telling her what she needed to do? He hardly knew her. How dare he? "What are you saying?"

"You mean I shouldn't poke my nose into your affairs. Maybe you're right. But you make it my affair when you talk about giving me that house. Could I do a lot with it? Sure. But that's not the point here. The question is whether you're going to run from a problem."

Oh, that scalded. It scalded even more because it reminded her of her childhood, of her father, who had run from everything right into the bottom of a bottle.

She wasn't like that.

Was she?

She wanted to glare at him, almost hating him in that moment, because he had left her feeling emotionally naked. Why had he done that? It felt cruel.

When he spoke again, his voice was quiet. "Guess I was out of line. And probably wrong."

But he wasn't wrong, she admitted. As knotted up as her feelings were over all of this, she recognized that kernel of truth. She wanted to run from all of this, from facing her past, from dealing with that house and all the memories it evoked. Except for the threat of taxes pursuing her down the years, or fines for code violations, she'd have ignored the entire situation.

This man, who had known her for such a very short time, had somehow looked all the way to her soul, to one of the most private places inside her. It was unnerving.

It was also embarrassing. She thought of herself as reasonably strong, having survived so much in previous years, including the death of both her parents. Now she was staring a huge weakness in the face and wondering if *that* had been the reason she had believed herself to be a sturdy survivor. Because she fled from all the difficult things?

Gah. Hiding in the museum with ancient bones and colleagues for company was a nice little hermitage, she admitted. Yes, she loved her work wholeheartedly, but she allowed little time for anything else...like a life.

Maybe some reevaluation was in order—but not right now. First she had to deal with the Higgins house, whether she wanted to or not. Tim was right. She couldn't run from this one.

It'd be nice, though, if she could. Just head back to Albuquerque and work and forget all about the house and the town she had been raised to think of as judgmental.

But whose judgment? It was beginning to seem as if that were her dad's. She had absolutely no reason to think poorly of this town. She hadn't met anyone but Tim and Earl yet, but both seemed nice. Particularly since Earl appeared to know the whole sordid story. He'd been anything but judgmental. From his first phone call to tell her Higgins had left her the house, he'd been totally sympathetic about her concerns, her resentment and her anger. He'd also been totally honest about the position her uncle Bob had placed her in.

But whether she was being fair to the town or not, it remained that she had her own issues—issues that were coming starkly into light because of that damn house. And Tim's insight.

She leaned forward for a cookie, realizing that she was beginning to get hungry again. She wasn't used to being so physically active most days. Not shoveling-snow active, anyway. It had kicked up her appetite.

"Want me to make you a grilled cheese sandwich or something?" Tim asked. "Or will cookies be enough?"

She glanced over her shoulder at him, still leaning forward. "Reaching for a cookie means I'm starving?"

He laughed. "Not necessarily. Just trying to be a good host."

She turned then, still sitting on the edge of the couch, and gave him a smile. "You're being a wonderful host. You took in a stranger, and you make me feel like I belong here, just like you and Matthew. That's a gift."

"Is it?" He shrugged slightly. "Honestly, I couldn't imagine you staying in the Higgins house all by yourself especially during the storm. Big, empty place. You'd have had heat and water, but I can't testify to much else yet. It's been unoccupied for a long time. I'm concerned about the air in there. I'm going to have it tested. Once I got the heat going, I don't know what might get into the air with time, and while I've been leaving windows open while I work, you wouldn't be able to do that during this storm. Anyway, there I am, looking at a house that's barely getting back into livable state, and you, not knowing a soul here…how was I going to leave you there? What if the power went out? The heat wouldn't shut down but you wouldn't have a single light."

"That would have been spooky," she admitted.

"Spookier than your dream, probably. And once the storm really set it, you'd have nowhere to go to escape. Then there's the motel." He grimaced. "I don't know for sure, but I suspect the some of the truck drivers who got stuck there might think it was a great time to booze it up and have a party. A different kind of creepy for you."

"I'm sure. That even crossed my mind earlier. But you still didn't have to make me so welcome in your home. I'm grateful to you."

"You're welcome. I'm enjoying your company, and Matthew certainly is, too. I think he's got a thousand times more questions than he knows how to ask about dinosaurs."

And that reminded her. "I'm sorry I brought up a trip to the museum. That put you on the spot."

He shook his head a little. "He may forget all about it and move onto a new fascination. If he doesn't…well, he needs to go to places like that. It might have been easier to take him to the place here in Wyoming, but if he wants to go to your museum, maybe over spring break. My busiest time of the year is summer, so it's hard to get away. But in the spring? We could fly down and spend a few days."

"He'd love it," she assured him. "We've got more than dinosaurs to look at. All kinds of sciency things and habitats he can walk through. He might like being able to travel back sixty-five million years in time and feel as if he's really there."

"I'm sure he'd like it."

"We have interactive displays, too, where he could try things out." Then she caught herself. "I sound like a travel brochure."

"That's okay. I was enjoying it." His dark gray eyes seemed to dance. "You're making me want to visit, too. However, with a boy that age…for all I know, next year he'll be begging to go to Cooperstown."

She leaned back, nibbling on her cookie. "It's true, I guess. I've seen kids go on and off dinosaurs pretty fast. We have summer programs and after-school programs, and I hear from the leaders that kids are always changing which program they want to be in. They kind of flea-hop around, thirsty for new things all the time."

His smile changed subtly, and something about the shift made her heart skip and a drizzle of purely sexual hunger run through her. What was different?

But it was as if the very air had changed. From talking about the museum to this? She must be imagining it. After all, she'd been fighting her attraction to him since they'd met—a whole day and a half ago. Too soon, too fast.

And maybe that very thing would make it safe, said a portion of her traitorous mind. How much threat could there be in something that would be over almost before it started?

"So…" He drew the word out. "You know I'm widowed. But what about you? Husband? Boyfriend? Girlfriend?"

"None of the above," she answered, trying to sound flip but instead hearing her own voice come out on the husky side, revealing entirely too much.

Then, almost as quickly as the air had started to turn

smoky with desire, he swept it away. "I always thought it was good to be happy on your own before getting involved with someone. Less neediness."

Well, he was probably right about that, but where was this coming from? "What are you trying to say, Tim?"

He shook his head a little as his expression grew almost rueful. "I think I'm trying to avoid taking this moment to places it shouldn't go. We only met yesterday, and I don't want you—or me, for that matter—to regret you accepting my hospitality. You should be safe here."

"What if I feel safe?" she asked impulsively. Her cheeks heated almost instantly with embarrassment.

"Then tell me that again in a few days. Now about tomorrow... I want to give you a really good tour of the house. We can talk about how much you want to do before you have to get back home. How much is essential and how much might help with selling it."

All business again. Somehow she felt as if she'd just lost an important opportunity. Surprisingly, the loss made her ache.

In the morning, there was no escaping the return to reality. She rode along with Tim when he took Matthew to school, but then they headed to the Higgins house.

"Matthew's a real pistol," she remarked.

"A constant joy," he agreed.

Then silence fell, mainly because she felt tension winding around her, stretching her nerves. No matter how hard she tried to tell herself it was just a house, that it was not some kind of living beast that could attack her, she was afraid of the memories it might evoke, so it might as well have been alive. Or haunted.

Usually she could look back over her past with a reasonable amount of objectivity. Time had passed, and she had grown up, the loss of her parents no longer as fresh. Yes, she still grieved for them, but the grief had grown quieter. And in the case of her father, the anger had gradually worn away. He'd been a crushed man, and while drowning himself in alcohol had been stupid and cruel to those he loved, he'd been a mortal and had succumbed. People made mistakes. It wasn't easy to recover from some of them.

So the man had made two huge mistakes in his life. He'd completely trusted a lifelong friend, and then he'd tried to wash away that mistake in alcohol. Even his few attempts at AA had failed.

He couldn't live with himself.

And that's what the Higgins house signified to her now. Adulthood had helped her to gain some understanding of the mechanisms that had affected her life, but it hadn't quite relieved her of all the fallout.

Even now she would unexpectedly turn a corner in life and be drawn up short as she realized she was facing a scar from the past. She hadn't walked through all of that untouched. She'd have to be insensate not to respond to the difficulties and wounds.

But the important thing was that she deal with it, get this job done and return to her life. While she tended to be solitary outside work, she had a great time at work and with her colleagues. Relating on a professional level was comfortable—comfortable enough that sometimes she went out to lunch or after work with a couple of people. But it didn't extend beyond that.

The house loomed before them as Tim turned into

the driveway. Memories couldn't hurt her, she reminded herself. So why was she so unnerved? Because the place would remind her of a brief time when her life had been full and happy, and how that had been so suddenly ripped from her.

Ludicrous. She'd dealt with that. She was beginning to feel like a whiny child.

The house smelled different from when she'd first entered it two days ago. Evidently the heat had warmed it through and through, and maybe had pulled old odors out of the walls. It was definitely musty, but she thought she could detect the aroma of Bob's cigars.

"Oh, man," she murmured as she stood inside.

"What?"

"Can you smell the cigars? Bob had one going all the time. I guess the smell is in the walls."

"Probably in the furniture, too. I presume you're going to get rid of it. After twenty years in an unregulated environment, I'm not sure it's any good anymore."

"I certainly don't want any of it." Most assuredly. The couch in the living room—she remembered jumping on it with Bob's daughter Millie, until they'd both been scolded. The rug had provided an area where they built towns and drove toy cars or set up tea parties for their dolls.

The kitchen was no better. She'd eaten a lot of home-made cookies in there. And upstairs were bedrooms where she'd played or sometimes spent the night. Even the backyard was haunted with memories of barbecues when Bob would invite a lot of his clients. Or his marks, if she were honest about it.

"Let's gut it," she said abruptly.

Tim looked askance at her. "Do you mean that? Really?"

"Gut it," she said again. "This whole town will be better for losing every possible memory of Bob Higgins. I mean, even his wife left him and changed her last name. The kids, too, I think I heard." She stepped farther inside. "If we can do it, I want to erase every mark in here that Higgins left behind."

He gave a low whistle. "That could get expensive."

"He left me some money. Earl advised me to keep it until I caught up with expenses. I just wanted to give it away, but maybe he was right. If I possess some of his ill-gotten gains, how much better if I use it to erase his existence?"

At that, a laugh escaped Tim. "Check. Erase Bob Higgins. Maybe we can do it without bankrupting you if you want to help."

"I've got a couple of weeks of vacation. I was planning to use most of it for a skiing trip in the mountains back home, but I could use it for this." She felt a smile spring to her lips. "You know, I think it would give me a great deal of satisfaction."

He shook his head a little, but his smile remained. "And to think I was trying to budget for minimal repairs to make the place pass an inspection for sale. Now you want to go whole hog?"

"As much as I can. I'll be thrilled, for example, if I never have to smell that cigar again."

He chuckled. "All right. We'll go room by room and make a list. If you really want to gut this place, though, the first thing we need to do is get the furnishings out. It'll make the rest of the work easier. But still, we need to spend a few hours checking it all out to see what's worth donating and what just needs a one-way trip to the county dump."

"Fair enough." Mentally she rolled up her sleeves. "I should have brought a way to mark things or list them."

"I've got stuff I left in the kitchen." He paused. "Or we can hold a sale on Saturday, let folks come by and browse and buy anything they want for a dollar or two. That might get you a little money to add to the kitty for cleaning this place out."

"You think anyone would want this stuff?"

He shrugged. "The mattresses wouldn't attract any interest. But a bed frame? Maybe that dining room table? The wood still appears to be in good shape. Anyway, some of it might appeal to people. Then we go through what's left and decide what might make a good donation. It could save you moving and haulage costs, if nothing else."

That sounded good to her. "But won't it hold up progress if we leave the furnishings until the weekend?"

"I suggest we move most of it into one or two rooms. Then we can work on the rest." He pulled a cell phone out of his pocket. "Let me see if I can get a couple of my buddies over to help out."

As she stood looking at the big, heavy sofa that was probably almost a hundred years old, she thought that was a great idea.

Vanessa was amazed by how fast things happened. Four of Tim's friends showed up, one of them with a big box truck, and soon furniture was moving. Some of the items went right into the box truck for a trip to the dump. The rest wound up gathered in the living and dining rooms, with a bit of spillover into the hallway.

When Bob's wife had left, she must have taken every item of real value from the house, while leaving the furniture behind. A move on the cheap. They did, however, run across a closet and dresser full of a man's clothes.

"Donate," argued Tim. "Plenty of people truly need clothes in decent condition. They won't know it's Bob's stuff."

"Probably not," she agreed. The clothes were fairly nondescript and could have been owned by anyone. "They need to be washed, though. The cigar smell is strong."

"There's a washer in the basement. I think it still works. Shall we find out?"

With the moving done, they were once again alone in the house together, and the afternoon had begun to fade into the season's early twilight.

"Your friends really helped a lot," she remarked as she and Tim put the clothes in plastic trash bags to carry downstairs. "They should send me a bill."

"They won't. It's the kind of thing friends do."

She'd never tested her friendships that far. If the thought had ever crossed her mind, she'd have been sure no one would have time or want to. Interesting. Maybe she needed to think about what that meant about her, not her friends.

Tim sensed that Vanessa was experiencing some kind of inner turmoil beyond being expected to deal with a house she'd never wanted to see again. Since she didn't bring it up, however, he let it rest. How could he ask, anyway? He hardly knew her and didn't have the right.

Since it was time for Matthew to be coming home from school, he suggested they leave the laundry for morning. She was agreeable and appeared eager to see Matthew again.

Ha, he thought with silent laughter. His son had a better way with the ladies than he did.

The circle in front of the school was filled up with parents' cars, while the bus circle at the side was beginning to move out. Matthew came running toward them as they eased into the circle, but he was not alone. Tim recognized Ashley McLaren, the fourth-grade teacher, and right behind her Julie Archer, the kindergarten teacher. Since Matthew was quite definitely in the second grade, Tim waited to see what they had to say.

"I wonder if Matthew got into something he shouldn't have. Why else would two teachers from other grades be coming with him?"

"I…" Vanessa's tentative answer broke off as Matthew opened the front door on her side and said, "Ms. Archer and Ms. McLaren know you, Vannie."

Tim's gaze leaped to Vanessa's face, and he saw huge uncertainty there. Also a passing urge to flee.

"Vannie!" exclaimed Julie. "My gosh, it's been years. You remember us? Julie Ardlow and Ashley Granger? We used to hang together a whole lot at school."

For a few seconds Vanessa appeared totally at a loss, then she summoned a smile. "I remember you," she said. "Sort of. It's been so long."

"It's been way too long. So when we found out you were in town from Matthew…"

The boy was already climbing behind her into the crew seat.

"We decided," Ashley interrupted Julie, "that we've got to get together. Just for coffee if you don't have time for more. Or maybe lunch. And I've got an additional request. Matthew says you work with dinosaur bones at a museum. If I beg nicely, will you come talk to my class? I'm sure they'd love it."

Tim almost smiled, but smothered the expression. He could sense both Vanessa's shock and her reluctance, but there were two bright-faced women from her past making friendly overtures. She was going to get reeled in by simple courtesy, and he couldn't help but think that would be good for her.

Then he started wondering what else Matthew had been talking about. It might be time to teach the boy that what happened at home stayed at home. He'd never felt the need before, but Vanessa's privacy had been pierced without her permission. For all he knew, she might be furious about this by the time they drove away.

But for now she was smiling, assuring Julie and Ashley that she'd love to meet for coffee, but she'd have to figure out when she could. "I'm clearing out the old Higgins house," she offered by way of explanation.

"I heard that man deeded his house to you," Ashley said. "I didn't know whether to be indignant. I thought for sure you'd just sell it without even looking at it."

"Earl Carter said I had some things to do first."

"I guess he'd know." Julie shrugged. "Anyway, give me a call when you can find an hour or so. Or if you want help dealing with the house, I'm sure we could find some time."

"We're freezing these folks," Ashley said. "The inside of that truck must feel like a meat locker. We'll let you go, but we're not hard to find. And let me know about talking to my class, okay?"

Tim felt the silence almost acutely as they at last eased from the circle and headed toward his home. "Sorry about that," he said after a few seconds.

"Did I do something wrong?" Matthew asked, apparently rediscovering his ability to chatter. "I was just talking about Vannie and how she works with dinosaur bones. Everyone was jealous that I get to talk to her. That was all."

"From little seeds big things grow," remarked Tim. "Did you ask Vanessa if it was okay to talk about her?"

Matthew grew uncharacteristically silent. Then, "Wasn't it? Is it some kind of secret?"

Oh, man, Tim thought. How was he going to explain the difference between secrets and confidentiality? About not talking about people without their permission? Especially when the person in question had a job that fascinated him.

"It's okay," Vanessa said. "It's okay. He didn't do anything wrong."

But maybe he had, Tim thought, shooting her another glance as he cornered into his driveway. Vanessa had lost her peppy look and appeared to have begun brooding. Well, when he could get Matt off to bed, he was going to ask her about her reaction.

But something else happened first. Vanessa climbed out into ankle-deep snow. Matthew tumbled out after her. All of a sudden she gasped.

"What?" Tim hurried out from behind the wheel and around the front of his truck.

Vanessa had bent over and was scooping snow into her bare hands. "You little brat. I didn't bring gloves."

But just as his heart froze with shock, he realized she had begun to laugh. A round circle of snow powdered her jeans, and a second later she had hurled a snowball back at Matt. Shrieking with laughter, the boy ducked and ran.

Tim leaned against the side of his truck to watch and see how far this went. It couldn't last long, given Vanessa was making snowballs with her bare hands, but it lasted for a few minutes, anyway. Snowballs flew back and forth, with Matthew giggling like mad and Vanessa laughing.

But at last Vanessa held up both her hands. "You win, Matthew. My hands are frozen now."

He came hurrying over, still grinning. "I'm sorry. That was fun. Maybe you should get some gloves."

"I have some, but not on me. Warn me beforehand next time."

Tim walked with the two of them into the house and immediately turned on the hot water tap. "Try to thaw your hands," he suggested to Vanessa as she pulled off her jacket. "Man, your fingers are red."

"My own fault," she said cheerfully. "I could have called quits sooner. But that was fun. Thanks, Matthew."

Tim began boiling water for hot chocolate and sent Matt to change into play clothes and to get ready to do his homework.

"I'm sorry," he remarked.

"For what?"

"Matt inadvertently put you on the spot. Maybe you didn't mind running into Ashley and Julie, but to be asked to give a presentation on dinosaurs?"

"He didn't put me on that spot. Ashley did." She turned off the hot water and dried her hands on the nearby kitchen towel. "That feels better."

"I'm sure Ashley would understand if you tell her you can't give a presentation."

She sat at the table and put her chin in her hand. "It's weird."

"What is?" He waited, hoping he was about to learn more about this complex woman. Behind him, he heard the quiet vibration as the pot began to simmer.

"I didn't want to see anyone when I came back to this town. I was afraid of the judgment. I think I told you. Anyway, I just ran into two of my oldest friends. They were friendly. I survived. But I can barely remember them."

He nodded. It wasn't surprising, considering she'd left at the age of seven. If he hadn't lived here his entire life, there were loads of people he'd probably have trouble remembering. For that matter, except for Matthew, he doubted Ashley and Julie would have recognized Vanessa. "I think you could walk these streets in almost perfect anonymity if you want. As long as Matthew zips his lip."

She shook her head a bit. "He really didn't do anything wrong. He was excited about dinosaurs or he probably wouldn't have said much. I get it."

"But where does that leave you?" he asked. Damn, this felt awkward. His son had blurted something totally innocent, but in the process had exposed this woman to something she'd been trying to avoid. The fact that it had gone well didn't mean it was okay. Vanessa hadn't planned to stay more than a couple of days, now she was talking about giving up her vacation to erase every sign of Bob Higgins from that house, then into her life had walked two people when she'd been trying to avoid facing anyone in this county.

Because of a fear she really didn't need to feel. How could anyone blame a little girl for any of what had happened? But her father had turned the area into a bugaboo for her, making her expect horrible reactions.

He poured hot water into cocoa mix in three mugs. One he placed in front of her before taking a second into the dining room, where Matt was pulling papers and a workbook out of his backpack.

"Did I do something wrong, Daddy?" he asked as he slid onto the chair in front of his homework. The mug of hot chocolate went onto a corner of the place mat.

"Not a thing," Tim said after a moment. Really, was this the kind of issue he wanted to use to demonstrate that families had to have some privacy? In this town, unless you kept your mouth shut, it wasn't long before everyone knew everything that was going on in your life. Since little of it needed to be secret, that was okay. But there were always things people wanted to keep private, from personal disagreements to the size of their bank accounts. Matthew would have to learn, but maybe not today.

Vanessa had been shocked, but she didn't seem overly disturbed that two old friends had found her. Maybe, when she got used to the idea, it would even make her feel more comfortable here.

He wanted that. He was surprised how much he wanted that. Mentally it put him back on his heels. There was no way she would stay here, he wasn't in a position to move to another state and try to find construction work, and he didn't want to uproot Matthew anyway. So of all possible women he could get truly interested in after all these years, he might be picking exactly the wrong one.

If he was. He smothered a sigh as he went back to the kitchen to start dinner. He didn't want Vanessa to hear it and ask if something was wrong. He was drawn to her. Sexually, of course, but it was more than that. In the short time he had known her, he'd sensed a kernel of true sorrow inside her, hidden behind the walls she seemed to erect against the rest of the world. But he didn't know her well enough to judge even that.

He just knew that she was fascinatingly complex, like a puzzle he wanted to solve, and that he sensed she was withdrawn in some truly important ways. Why?

And why did he care? She was just passing through.

At least today might have taught her she had nothing to dread in this town.

Chapter Five

When he reached the kitchen, Vanessa was still sitting there, cradling her cup of hot chocolate with both hands. Her face revealed nothing at all, smooth as an unused canvas although a pretty heart shape, until she noticed he was there. Then a smile sprang to her lips. "Woolgathering," she said.

"Sometimes a productive thing to do. Anything useful?"

"Maybe." She paused, and he didn't question her while he sat with his own cocoa. He waited silently, giving her any time or space she needed, room to follow a different line of thought if she chose.

A few minutes later, however, she surprised him. "I'm beginning to wonder how bent I still am because of my upbringing."

"I'm sorry? What do you mean?"

"Oh, I don't know. My dad filling me with anger, for one thing. I thought I'd left that behind. His alcoholism. But I don't think that's even the worst of it. We moved constantly because he drank. He lost one job after another, and I wound up always being the new girl wherever we went. I never made real friends, first because I didn't have time, and second because I figured I'd be gone in a few months. I'm beginning to wonder if I'm still living that way."

There was no answer for that, of course. At least not from him. Impulsively, he reached across the table and rested his fingertips on the back of her hand. She didn't pull away, much to his relief, but the almost physical jolt of electricity he felt when he touched her warned him that his desire for her was growing rapidly. Dangerous ground, he reminded himself. She'd showed no interest in him, maybe because she didn't feel the attraction, or maybe because of what she had just been talking about.

She'd made herself sound as if she were living behind high emotional walls because of the way she had grown up. Maybe so. He doubted she was sure herself, merely questioning if something in her had been irrevocably changed by her past.

But wasn't everyone affected by their past? He knew he was. The loss of his wife had seared grief deep into his soul, had left him with a loneliness that nothing could erase. His life was full—he had his son, whom he dearly loved—but he no longer had Claire. She'd been a bright and shining spot, and her death had left a blackened crater in her place.

He dated rarely; he pursued no relationship with any woman. Why? Because he was afraid? Or because he felt it would be some kind of betrayal of Claire? Or maybe both. If he couldn't sort that out, how could Vanessa sort out all the things her childhood had done to her?

Did it have to be sorted out? As the thought occurred to him, he spoke it. "Why are you wondering? Does it matter if you're content?"

"I'm wondering if I'm content." She surprised him by turning her hand over and clasping his fingers. "Let me ask you. You were terribly wounded by the loss of your wife, I'm sure. Are you content with the way things are?"

What a devil of a question, he thought, staring at their clasped hands. Content? In a way he supposed he was. But that was a long way from what he'd had before. He and Claire hadn't been deliriously happy all the time, or even much of the time. Life didn't allow that. But he'd been happier than he was now. More content. "It's not the same," he said finally.

"I'm sure it isn't," she admitted. She squeezed his hand almost gently, then withdrew hers. "I'm just wondering how it is that I manage to avoid feeling deeply for anyone. I've been at the museum for a few years now. I ought to be settled. I ought to have a crowd. But there's a part of me that never connects beyond the surface. As if I'm guarded all the time. Is that normal? I somehow doubt it."

He frowned. "Not everyone's the same. Some people are introverts. Maybe that's all it is for you. Are you thinking you're not normal?"

"I'm thinking that maybe I don't know what normal is."

He shook his head. "I'm not sure there is one." He

was beginning to ache for her again, sensing some kind of sorrow in her that she was struggling to come to grips with. He hadn't the faintest idea how to help. No words of wisdom. Life for him was a constant round of just getting by and being grateful for what he did have. If it wasn't enough, then too bad. The feeling would pass.

She spoke after a couple of minute. "Meeting Julie and Ashley today—like I said, I barely remember them. It was such a long time ago, and I was so young. But… what if I'd stayed here? Grown up with them? They're obviously so comfortable together, and they seem to still be friends. Would I have been like that? On the inside rather than always on the outside?"

Oh, man. "You're talking to a building contractor here," he reminded her. "Good with the hands, but not so much with the brains."

"Oh, cut it out," she said almost irritably. "Admittedly, I haven't known you long, but you don't strike me as stupid. Not even a little."

"Well, then, you're walking into territory I'm not competent to deal with."

Her mouth curved in one corner. "You think I need therapy?"

"Not for me to say. Just thinking that you're talking about something I can understand, but I don't have any way of responding that might be useful."

"But you understand?"

She looked almost eager, he realized. She needed something, and he just wished he knew what it was and how to provide it. Seven-year-olds were easy for the most part. Adults not so much. "I miss my wife," he said. "I'm not looking for a replacement. In fact, that would be impossible. And I guess I've kinda been avoiding getting involved again. Maybe I'm afraid because losing Claire was so painful."

She nodded. "I can understand that. I don't blame you for being afraid, either. I'm just wondering if I'm experiencing the same thing in a different way. So many losses over the years until finally I gave up. But maybe not. Maybe this is who I would have been if I'd always lived here and grown up with my friends."

He couldn't answer that, obviously, and she didn't seem to expect him to. She might be right, though. Examining the detritus his loss had left in its wake, he could only wonder about experiencing the same thing repeatedly. He'd probably become some kind of hermit. Well, except for Matthew. Matthew had kept him going through the darkest days. From what she'd so far said, Vanessa had nothing. Both her parents had evidently failed her, leaving her insecure and lost as a child.

She'd been avoiding looking at him directly, except for brief glances, as if she was afraid of even that much connection. But then, surprising him, her gaze fixed on his. In her mossy-green eyes, he read hunger. But hunger for what? The kind of connection she'd evidently been missing her whole life? Or something else? Passion? He sure felt a strong need for sex with her himself, but he was old enough to know such things passed and could easily make a mess. He was sure she didn't want that. No more messes, no more losses. After all, he was avoiding that himself.

But something about Vanessa was special. He just wished he could put his finger on what drew him, apart from her beauty. Her loneliness? That wasn't a great place to start. Two lonely souls wouldn't necessarily be good for each other.

Why was he even thinking like this, anyway? She'd be going home soon enough. Did he want another hole in his life? Absolutely not.

He heard someone knocking on the door. A glance at the clock told him it was only a few minutes past nine. Late for a neighborly call, maybe, but not too late. Or it could be one of his customers. Occasionally one would get a bug about something in the evening after looking over progress on the job or thinking over a proposal for work and call or drop by. Although in this weather, dropping by seemed like the least preferable choice.

He rose, excusing himself, and went to find out who was there. A young man he knew mostly by sight was standing there. Larry Crowley, he believed.

"Hey, Tim," the young man said. "I heard Vanessa Welling is here. We were in school together when we were kids. I spent some time at her dad's ranch. Is she around?"

Tim eyed him, seeing a pleasant-looking young man with a smile. Average height and build. "Kinda late for a social call," he remarked. Not that he had any right to prevent Vanessa from seeing anyone.

"Yeah, sorry. You probably don't know because I'm not around town a lot, but I'm a long-haul trucker. Gotta leave again at dawn."

Instead of letting the frigid night swallow all the heat from his house, Tim invited Larry inside. "I'll see if she has a minute," he said, leaving Larry in the small foyer.

"Thanks. If not, just tell her I said hi."

"Okay." He walked back to the kitchen. Vanessa was sitting upright in her chair. She must have been listening.

"Larry Crowley, old friend?" he questioned. "Just wants to say hi before he leaves again."

She blinked, evincing surprise. "Larry?"

He watched her search her memory, then she nodded. "Amazing. Julie and Ashley surprised me, but someone else? I *do* vaguely remember him, though. He liked playing with cars in the dirt."

Tim could have laughed. That sounded like a kid. "Did you play with him?"

"Sometimes." She rose, put on a smile and walked out to the foyer.

He hesitated near the kitchen door, letting her have her moment with an old friend. Listening. Why he felt edgy he couldn't have said.

"Larry," she said. "It's been ages."

"Yeah. You're looking good."

"So are you."

Tim relaxed. Then the bomb dropped.

Vanessa had only the vaguest memory of Larry Crowley, a very young boy covered in dust with a passion for tiny metal cars. She had one or two images of him at her parents' ranch, but none of him from school. Maybe one at Bob's house? She wasn't sure.

Now she faced a thin man of about her age, with shaggy dark hair and eyes that held no warmth. Just as uneasiness began to prickle along her nerves, he spoke.

"My dad's dead."

"I'm sorry," she answered, taken aback. "Mine, too."

"Yeah, I heard. He helped Higgins steal my dad's retirement. Nothing left. Your whole family stinks!"

She took a step back, startled and suddenly afraid. Her dad's constant warnings about judgment came back to her, and she couldn't help retorting, "We lost everything, too, Larry. Everything."

"My dad always said your dad was the reason—"

Suddenly Tim was there, inserting himself between the two of them. "I think you ought to go, Larry."

"But her father—"

"She wasn't responsible for any of that. She was a kid, just seven. How old were you? Could you have stopped your dad from doing anything? Yelling at Vanessa won't do any good, but it'll sure as hell make me madder than a wet hornet. Now leave!"

Larry was clenching and unclenching his fists. He glared at Vanessa and Tim before turning and storming out.

As if from a great distance, Vanessa watched Tim close and lock the door. Tremors had begun to run through her, and her face felt like a frozen mask.

Her dad had warned her. For years he'd claimed this town would sit in judgment. She'd dropped her guard because of Julie and Ashley. Way too easily.

Slowly her hands came up, and she wrapped her arms around herself. "I've got to leave in the morning," she said shakily. "Do whatever the house needs. Drop a bomb on it. I don't care."

The urge to flee to privacy overwhelmed her, and she turned to go to the bedroom. Before she took a step, strong arms wrapped around her from behind and held her tightly.

"Easy," Tim murmured. "Easy. Just one jerk—"

"Saying what everyone thinks!"

"Saying what *he* thinks," Tim corrected firmly. "Sounds like his life was poisoned the same way yours was, by an angry father. That doesn't mean either man was right."

"I don't want to stay in this town," she argued, gradually regaining her strength. "I don't need any more of that."

He turned her, making her face him, enclosing her once more in his embrace. "It'll be okay. First of all, I'm damn near positive that you won't meet another soul like Larry. But even if you do, I'll be there. I promise. I'm not going to stand for that crap from anyone. How idiotic can you get? Like a seven-year-old girl could have anything to do with what happened? Most people have more brains than that."

"But I'm the only one they have left to yell at."

"Larry's a jackass. You're not responsible, and yelling at you for something other people did is downright stupid and cruel. It's a good thing he's on his way out of town in the morning, or I'd hunt him up and tell him a thing or two."

Surprise began to trickle through Vanessa as she listened to Tim. He was indignant for her. Angry on her behalf. Ready to protect her against the things she feared. And angry at Larry, while all she felt was awful pain. Shouldn't she be angry, too?

The feeling of being protected, however, warmed her somewhere deep inside. She'd never felt that way before, and however temporary it was, it came like a revelation. Someone could actually be concerned enough to take care of her.

"You're kind," she murmured, letting her head come to rest on his shoulder, letting tension seep out of her.

"I'm mad," he said. "There was no call for that. None at all. No one he should be angry with is in this house. Damn him."

"His father…"

"To hell with his father. To hell with yours, too, for that matter. Two grown men made big mistakes, and they're going to dump it on *your* head? I am completely out of patience."

A shiver passed through her, but this one wasn't uncomfortable. She leaned into the man, grateful for his strength. She had always thought herself strong, but she was beginning to see it differently. Not strong, but hiding. Now she'd been forced out of hiding, and she couldn't handle Larry's anger. Some strength.

Matt's voice came from upstairs. "Daddy?"

"What are you doing up?"

"I heard a man. Is Vannie okay?"

"She will be. Don't worry, son. You can give her a hug in the morning, if you want."

"Okay."

She faintly heard the sound of bare feet in the upstairs hall. "He's a good kid," she said, her voice thick. Only then did she feel that her eyes were burning with unshed tears. Tears for what? Was she having a breakdown of some kind? Maybe coming back here had been the worst thing she could possibly have done.

But with Tim's arms around her, she couldn't quite believe that.

"Come on," he said quietly. "Let's go sit in the living room. Maybe have a cookie, or I can reheat your cocoa. You must have had an adrenaline rush, and that burns calories fast."

Was that why she had started shaking? Maybe. She really didn't know. The attack had been unexpected, coming out of nowhere, it seemed, despite all her father's warnings. A man calling himself an old friend had suddenly turned into a threat.

"He wasn't a threat," she said slowly, mostly to herself, as Tim kept his arm around her shoulder and walked her into the living room.

"A threat to your peace of mind. I don't believe he'd have gotten violent."

"I don't think so." Not now. But had she? For a few moments there, she'd felt real fear. A gut certainty that Larry wanted to hit her. Probably a misreading of his body language, because he had certainly been angry. "He must be really seething that he didn't get to have his say."

Tim let go of her and motioned her to sit on the sofa. "Too bad. You will never be the person he needs to say it to. Now, do you want fresh cocoa or some cookies?"

Her stomach had knotted. Putting something in it had become necessary. "Milk and cookies?" she suggested. A childhood treat that had suddenly arisen in her mind, promising comfort. A different kind of comfort from what she had felt in Tim's arms. How could a man's hug have reached her so deeply, bringing warmth to the corners of her soul?

"Coming up."

Her thoughts drifted upward to Matthew, and she hoped he hadn't heard any of that ugly confrontation.

He'd obviously been worried, and that troubled her. Maybe she should move into the Higgins house until she could leave. She didn't want Matthew exposed to that kind of ugliness, not even briefly. He was such a bright and happy little guy. She hoped that never changed, although given the way life operated, it probably would, but she didn't want it to be soon, or because of her.

Tim returned with a tray bearing a plate of cookies, two glasses of milk and some paper napkins. "Dig in," he said cheerfully. "Dip if you like. Isn't that half the fun of cookies and milk?"

"Clearly you have a child."

He laughed. "Seems like. I'd quit dipping years ago because of drippy mess I always made, then he taught me that it didn't matter because it was so enjoyable. Makes me feel like a kid again, and you know, the mess isn't that hard to clean up."

She smiled and reached for a chocolate cookie and the glass of milk. Then, almost daringly, she dipped the cookie and quickly ate the soaked part.

"Yum," he said, then dipped a cookie for himself. "So, are you unwinding from our visitor?"

"Yeah, but I feel awful because Matthew might have heard some of that."

"I doubt it. He came because he heard something, but I'm pretty sure it was seeing me hugging you that made him wonder if something was wrong. If he *did* happen to hear anything Larry said, we'll talk about it tomorrow."

She swallowed another bite of cookie, washing it down with more milk. The whole thing with the cookies and milk was soothing. Tim made quick work of his cookie and set his glass on the coffee table.

"You and Matthew have a wonderful relationship."

"I'm lucky."

"No, I think you're good. A good father."

He turned his head toward her as he rested his arm along the back of the couch, and she was astonished to read something like sorrow on his face. "I'm sorry you missed that."

"Not in my early years," she said truthfully. "I don't have a lot of very clear memories from before, but I do remember feeling loved and secure. Bob Higgins blew that all up, so I can understand where Larry's coming from."

"That doesn't give him the right to dump it on you." Having said that as if it were indisputable, he fell silent, drumming his fingers on the back of the couch. "You're thinking about moving into the Higgins house, aren't you?"

His accuracy astonished her. She hadn't said a word about it. "What, do you read minds?"

"Faces, maybe." He looked at her. "Why? You'd be miserable and uncomfortable."

"Because I don't want Matthew to see anything like what just happened. I'd like to preserve his innocence as long as possible."

He smiled faintly. "Very kind of you. But innocence only lasts so long, and sometimes even at seven you have to deal with the way things are. You certainly ought to know that. Matthew's had his share of playground dustups and broken friendships. The innocence is bound to get chipped away. We just hope it's not in some awful, shattering way. But eventually it will be. That's life."

"But..."

RACHEL LEE

He silenced her with a shake of his head. "I doubt he would have even understood what Larry was saying, beyond that he was angry with you. Matthew is perfectly able to understand people getting angry. He's even been known to do it himself sometimes."

His words seemed to release a pressure valve inside her, and she relaxed with a quiet laugh. "Point made."

"Yeah, he can become a little tempest sometimes. Not often. I'm blessed with a son who is usually happy. But once in a while, not so much. We've butted heads a few times."

"I find that hard to imagine."

"He has a mind of his own." Tim shrugged. "I don't want to stifle it, but occasionally I have to object. Depending on how determined he is, it can become quite something."

She could almost imagine Matthew standing stiffly, his face screwed up with anger, probably looking more adorable than frightening. "I feel sorry for Larry."

"Really?"

"He grew up with the same kind of stuff I did. I can imagine the bitterness his father must have felt and expressed countless times. Heck, I don't have to imagine it. I lived it. It has an effect."

"Of course. But do you go around taking it out on other people?"

"Maybe only because I don't have someone to take it out on. Bob was in prison. Now he's dead. Maybe I would have wanted to do exactly what Larry did."

He drummed his fingers again briefly. "I don't read you that way, but I could be wrong. I don't know you very well yet. Still, I don't see it. Larry's anger is mis-directed. What have you done with yours?"

She put down her glass then leaned her head back against the couch and closed her eyes. "I think I buried it. I know as I got older I grew really angry with Bob, and with my dad, too, but for different reasons. I was mad because Bob hurt my parents, of course. But I was mad at my dad for his drinking and losing every job he had, which upset my mother until she looked ninety when she wasn't yet forty. I think Dad did that to her more than the loss of the ranch."

His fingers moved from the back of the sofa to rest on her shoulder, stroking gently. Pleasant shivers ran through her even as she thought about a past that was ugly and had sometimes been nearly unbearable. God, his touch was magical, tugging her out of the ditch of memory.

"And you?" he asked yet again. "I'm not asking about your parents. I'm asking how you dealt with all of it."

"I survived," she said flatly. "That's all I could do. I survived. I pulled inside myself until nothing could touch me anymore."

In that instant she realized a home truth about her-self. She'd almost entirely squelched her emotional life to protect herself. She was barely more than half a person.

The recognition ripped something deep inside her, and the agony filled her. She'd not only hidden, she'd run, locking entire parts of herself away.

Jumping up, ignoring Tim when he called her name, she went back to the bedroom and closed the door. Leaning back against it, she stood shaking, horrified and agonized as she faced the real loss she had suffered.

Herself.

Chapter Six

Saturday morning came swiftly. The sale had been announced on the radio and in the local weekly, and despite the cold gray day, quite a number of people showed up to pick through the furnishings left behind by the Higgins family.

Vanessa had decided not to put prices on anything. She didn't care if she made a dime off this, so she sat in the kitchen and accepted whatever offers people made. Bit by bit the house began to empty itself of usable furnishings, and from her perspective the people who came were helping her out.

After Larry's visit, she was initially tense about this whole affair, but the people who came were friendly, and the majority didn't seem to have any idea who she was. Bob Higgins had faded into the background a long time ago for most, and the Welling name had vanished from the county twenty years ago. Older people who might have remembered simply smiled and welcomed her to town.

A very different reception from the one she had anticipated. A scandal that might have been on every tongue all those years ago had ceased to matter.

Maybe she ought to learn something from that, she thought. It was past. Long past. Now she needed to deal with the scars that had come after, and maybe place the blame where it really belonged: on her father, a man who had been unable to overcome his losses, and instead had lost himself and his family.

Look at Tim, she thought as he moved between rooms with Matthew nearby. He'd lost his wife yet had continued to make a good life for his son.

Her father clearly had a weakness of character, and after her realization the other night, she had to face the possibility that she might suffer from a similar weakness. Not as bad, obviously. She was maintaining a life and a job and had plenty of casual friends. But anything deeper than casual? She hid. Not in a bottle but inside herself.

Matthew eventually grew bored with wandering around the same rooms and watching people talk to his dad about furniture. He came to the kitchen to sit with Vanessa.

"How come you don't want this stuff?" he asked.

"Because I'm going to clean up the house and sell it. Furniture would get in the way."

He turned toward her, a frown creasing his young brow. "You're not going to live here?"

"That's not my plan," she said forthrightly.

He nodded slowly but didn't look exceptionally happy about it. "You have to go back to the museum."

"Yes, I do."

"But why can't you stay here?"

A million reasons. Many still to be sorted through. But there was one reason she thought he'd understand. "My job is too far away, kiddo. I'd have to fly back and forth, and I can't do that every day, or even every week."

He nodded again, gravely. "And we don't have a museum here."

"I'm afraid not."

"We can come visit you, though, right?"

Another bud of warmth blossomed in her heart. "You bet."

Another visitor approached, wanting to buy two end tables. Vanessa let them choose their own price, then suggested Matthew count the money and write it down on her list. That made the woman smile. "Cute boy," she said before walking away with her prizes.

Watching Matt carefully print the name of the item and the amount in the designated column, she felt a small shock of surprise. Were people paying more because she let them set their own price? Because the sum was mounting, and it was more than she had expected.

A little while later, Tim came into the kitchen to snag one of the sandwiches they'd brought with them and to give Matthew one, spread out on a napkin. Simple peanut butter.

"Tim? Do you think I made a mistake by not pricing anything?"

He pulled out the remaining chair and straddled it.

A table with only three chairs. That still struck her as strange. "Why do you ask?"

"Because people are paying far more than I expected."

The corners of Tim's eyes crinkled. "They're paying what they want to. If that makes them raise the price a little, I'm sure it's not by much. On the other hand, if you'd priced everything, no matter how low, they'd have felt obliged to haggle."

Maybe he had a point, she thought as Matthew asked what haggling was. Tuning out the explanation, noting only how patiently and clearly Tim explained, she wandered down a trail of thought triggered by Matthew.

He seemed to want her to stay. He professed understanding about why she couldn't, but had she detected a note of disappointment in his voice? Already he was planning to visit her? She wondered what Tim would think of that.

Of course, Matthew was only seven, and he could forget a lot before spring break or the summertime. He could get distracted.

Oddly enough, for someone who was an emotional recluse, she hoped he didn't forget. She genuinely liked the child. For that matter, she was growing fond of his father.

Dangerous territory for her, but she had a safety valve in her eventual departure. That date promised her security.

Apparently bargain hunters were early shoppers. The crowds died away until everyone was gone shortly after two. So was most of the furniture.

"One last truckload for donation or the dump," Tim

said. "Gee, that went well. I'm such a genius for thinking of it."

Matthew giggled.

"It was a brilliant idea," Vanessa said.

"And not too tough on you?"

She glanced at Matthew, wondering how much the
child had picked up and understood, then decided probably very little. "Not tough at all. Everyone was really
nice."

"And I helped," Matthew announced. "Does that
make me a genius, too?"

"Absolutely," said his father. "Define 'genius.'"

Matthew pursed his lips, then sighed. "I gotta use
the dictionary?"

"Always."

Matthew scowled. "That's like school."

"Precisely. Or homework, even. Okay, everyone,
jackets on. I want to air out this house one more time
before we go."

"You made it cold in here this morning," Matthew
said. "Do we have to do it again?"

"You won't care. We're leaving."

Matthew ran out into the yard to play in what was
left of the snow while Vanessa helped Tim open all the
windows.

"We're doing this why?"

"Because until the guy comes to test the air in here
on Monday, I have no idea what we might be breathing."

She nodded. "Still worried about lead?"

"Until I'm told otherwise, yes. Basically, since I first
aired it out, I doubt there's much bad in here. I was more
worried because the place had been shut up so long.

Now it's open a lot and it's probably safe. But if we find lead paint… I hate to tell you, Vannie, but that could get expensive, depending. I just hope the sagging paint is all latex, and the wallpaper isn't covering bad secrets."

"I never thought about all of this."

"No one ever does. We all live on assumptions."

An interesting statement, she thought as she finished opening the last upstairs windows. There was no mistaking that a strong, icy breeze was blowing through the house.

We all live on assumptions. She'd certainly brought a few of them along with her here. With the exception of Larry, she'd run into absolutely no judgment or hostility. The things her father had dreaded were mere boogeymen. At least so far.

Then it was time to close the windows, and once again she walked room to room with Tim.

"This will give us a great baseline reading on Monday," he said. "A house shut up for way too long—in this case almost two decades—can pick up a lot of bad things. Radon from the basement, for example. Most houses need a good airing from time to time, lead or no lead. So whatever the inspector reads on Monday should establish what someone living here would be exposed to. And what we might be exposed to as we strip it down."

"You suggested I stay here!" she said, pausing and staring at him.

He shrugged. "I didn't think you'd have a problem for a few days, not with me airing the place out again and again. And if you'd stayed here, I'd have kept on doing it. Come on, Vannie. You don't think I wanted to poison you!"

Horrified at what she had just suggested, wondering where that had come from, she leaned back against a papered wall and closed her eyes. Surely she didn't believe Tim would have exposed her to harm. So what had she been thinking? Or not thinking, was probably a better question. Was she acting on some gut instinct to make sure she didn't get involved? Because she was sure getting involved here, and her escape date suddenly didn't seem safe enough.

"Are you angry with me?" Tim asked when she didn't move or respond.

"No. Really, no. I don't know what I was thinking. I certainly don't believe you'd expose me to harm. And if I don't believe that about me, I definitely know you wouldn't bring Matthew here if you were concerned." She opened her eyes, shuddering a little as she tried to release tension. Really, she had to get over these hang-ups. Sometimes they made her act in stupid ways. Like this.

She and Tim resumed closing the windows. He looked thoughtful, however, and she was worried she'd offended him beyond repair. "I'm really sorry," she said as they closed the last of the windows.

Outside, Matthew had evidently found a couple of other children to play with him in the snow. Their piping, happy voices reached even through the closed windows.

"It's okay," he said.

She wasn't sure it was, but didn't know what else to

say. Trying to change subjects, she asked, "Does anyone call Matthew 'Matt'?"

"At school they do, I think. For me it's just an old habit. Claire and I did it when he was an infant. Big name for a little guy." He gave a brief laugh. "I don't think it's going to last much longer, though. He's going to decide what he prefers."

Back in the kitchen, Tim scooped the remaining cash into the bank envelope he'd brought for her to use, and passed it to her. She passed it right back.

"Down payment on everything you need to do here," she said. "Or at least a small start."

She summoned a smile then headed for the front door. A perfectly good day, and she'd made a mash of it. Well, that was certainly something she seemed to be good at. She ought to be locked up with her fossils.

Matthew was only slightly reluctant to head home. The kids he'd been playing with were friends from school, and they didn't live that far away. Tim had no problem promising there'd be more time to play with them while he was working on the house. That satisfied Matthew.

Vanessa wasn't such an easy puzzle. Her reaction, thinking that he might have let her stay in a house with poisonous air, had shocked him. Then he'd watched her expression alter and realized that it had shocked her, too.

The lady had some issues. He knew that, but now he'd gotten a taste of how deeply they ran. Far from simply fearing judgment over her father's past, she didn't seem to expect anyone to take care of her in any way. God, what a childhood she must have had. Vanessa

Welling against the world. Had her mother even filled in the gaps? He'd assumed so, but now he thought not. She must have practically raised herself in a lot of ways.

What a sorry couple of parents.

At home, he looked at his son's bright face and hoped he never failed that boy. Matthew deserved every unshadowed moment of childhood that life would allow. He deserved to feel safe and protected by his father. He deserved the magic and wonder of each new day.

But Tim wasn't a fool, and he knew he couldn't even guarantee that he'd always be there for Matthew. Claire had been stolen from them. Life happened to everyone.

But it battered some more than others, he supposed, although he was fond of saying that there was no way to tell what burdens another person carried. Nor could burdens be compared.

But he felt a deepening compassion for Vanessa. A lovely young woman who, the more he grew to know her, seemed to be very alone and locked up within herself. The only time she really loosened up was with Matthew.

He wished he could find a way to loosen the restraints life had locked her in, but he knew it wasn't his place and that it was also a dangerous pursuit. She'd built a life she felt mostly content with. Who was he to disturb the walls she'd built for survival?

Worse than that, he wasn't qualified to do so safely.

But that didn't keep him from feeling bad about it.

Let it rest, he told himself. She needed to resume her life in a week or two, and she wouldn't want to go home with her defenses full of holes. Who knew what she was dealing with back in Albuquerque?

Bones, yes. But he could also easily imagine some politics and possibly jockeying among the people working at the museum. Every workplace suffered from some of that.

Holding herself aloof might be the best protection she had. It must have been when she was a child.

So let her be. Ignore the impulse to dash in somehow like a white knight. And while he was at it, put away his desire for her.

Because that just kept nagging at him. He had some self-restraint, and while he occasionally caught a glimmer of interest in her smile or her eyes, he could easily be misreading her. And what if they had sex and it brought her walls down?

Even though he was a guy, he was aware that sex brought down some barriers. It had to. And Claire had once told him that women were especially susceptible to falling in love with a man when they'd had sex. He couldn't remember what the subject had been, but he clearly remembered her saying that. It kept his pants zipped most of the time.

He'd since gathered that not all women reacted that way. A couple of brief failed attempts at relationships had taught him that. Still…

Dang, he wished his parents were still around, especially his mother. He'd have loved to talk to her, to see what she thought of Vanessa and her barricades. Or even Claire's parents, who had utterly shocked him and probably half the town when they announced they were moving to New Zealand. Because of the *Lord of the Rings* movies.

Yeah, really. A couple of middle-aged Tolkien fans

on the adventure of a lifetime. When they called, they always promised Matthew that when he was old enough they were going to bring him to visit.

Which had resulted in the entire works of Tolkien being on his shelf. He'd read them start to finish to the boy and wondered if he'd be doing that again this winter.

Well, except they now had this Harry Potter thing going.

Tim sighed, looked at the time and realized that he hadn't even thought about dinner. Vanessa had gone to take a shower and said she needed to catch up on email. Matthew was settled in front of the TV playing a game that absolutely promised it contained no violence or graphic gore.

Taking a chance, he went down the hall to Vanessa's room, once his and Claire's room, and knocked.

After a few seconds, the door opened. Vanessa had turbaned a towel around her hair and was wearing a thick, fluffy green bathrobe.

"I was wondering," he said, his throat feeling suddenly tight and his voice sounding thick. "I need to run out and take care of dinner. Can you watch Matthew for maybe a half hour? He's in the living room playing a video game."

"Sure," she said with a smile. "Not a problem. Just let me get dressed."

As she closed the door, he walked away absolutely certain she hadn't been wearing a thing under that robe. His mouth turned as dry as the Gobi Desert.

Ah, hell.

It was cold enough on the run to Maude's diner to

chill his impulses and restore rational thought. *Man triumphs over hormones*, he thought with amusement as he walked inside and ordered dinner. He wasn't sure what Vanessa would like and had failed to ask her. Oversight. Duh.

But he ordered Matthew's favorite burger and fries with a side of veggies, then he ordered a grilled chicken sandwich for Vanessa and a steak sandwich for himself. He'd have no problem if she wanted to switch. Then, for safety's sake, a huge chef's salad.

"Feeding an army?" Maude asked.

"Screwup. I failed to ask what everyone wanted."

Maude harrumphed, her usual sour response to life. Thing was, her cooking made up for everything else. The diner was always busy, and everyone called it by her name, not its proper name, the City Diner.

Right now, except for a pizza place at the edge of town and the truck stop diner, she was the only game in town. Sometimes he wished they'd get some variety, but he doubted people around here had a lot to spend on eating out. Maude's was always cheap and always good. Who could compete?

By the time he got home, Vanessa was dressed in a tan chamois shirt and faded blue jeans, her damp hair caught in a narrow headband, and busy playing the game with Matthew. She sat cross-legged on the floor beside him, laughing at her own learning curve. Matthew was an expert, and it showed. Tim sometimes played the game with his son, and marveled at the boy's patience. It was as if he'd been born with a game controller in his hand.

"Hamburger?" Tim called from the entry. Matthew at once paused the game and jumped up.

"Let's eat, Vannie!"

She was still smiling broadly as she rose to her feet in one smooth movement without touching her hands to the floor. The woman must practice yoga, he thought as he continued into the kitchen. He was in pretty good shape, but he doubted he could have managed that.

Matthew knew the rules and didn't have to be reminded to eat his vegetables first. With plates on the table, Vanessa helped herself to a generous serving of the salad and only half of the chicken sandwich. Hardly surprising. Maude's portions were designed for hardworking men from the ranches. These days many carried home takeout containers. For lots of people around here, life had become more sedentary than in past times.

Matthew made conversation easily. "Do you ever dig up bones, Vannie?"

"I have a few times," she answered.

"Was it fun?"

"It was really exciting when I found something, but most of it..." She smiled. "It's hot, hard work most of the time, Matthew."

"Is that why you work in the museum?"

Tim almost laughed. Good question, though.

"Truthfully," Vanessa said, "I chose to work in the museum because I get to solve puzzles. For me that's more fun than finding the fossils."

Matthew swallowed some more of his hamburger before asking, "So it's boring to dig them up?"

"Not exactly." Vanessa paused. "It's hard to explain. I like the work. It's really exciting when you find something. But a lot of the time you're just brushing away dirt, and chipping at rock gently, hoping something will be there. You have to bring a lot of patience. What I do now? I'm excited most of the time."

"I still want to try finding some bones."

"Then you should. And when I get home, I'm going to send you some 3-D dinosaur puzzles."

"What are those?" His face lit with curiosity.

"You get a box full of thin wood cut in the shape of dinosaur bones, and a drawing of the dinosaur. You have to compare the puzzle pieces to a drawing of each kind of bone and then figure out where it belongs. When you get done, you'll have a dinosaur skeleton like in a museum."

Matthew beamed. "That sounds like fun."

"It definitely is. We have several different kits and I've tried them all. Cool stuff."

Tim thought he wouldn't mind trying one of them himself. The builder in him, he supposed. And a different kind of problem solving for Matthew.

After helping with cleanup, his son went back to his video game, leaving Vanessa and Tim in the kitchen with after-dinner coffee.

"I love that kid," she said unexpectedly.

"Easy to do." He smiled. "At least I think so."

"You wouldn't be wrong." Then, hoping he wasn't about to put his foot in it, he asked, "Your mother? You made her life sound very sad. Did you get lost in the shuffle?"

She lifted the teaspoon and stirred coffee that didn't need stirring. "She was overwhelmed. Sometimes she was working two jobs. Then with Dad's drinking problem, and him needing to move to find another job, she was always struggling herself. Finding a new job, making enough so she could squirrel some away for the next time he got fired. I told you how it aged her."

"I remember. But what about you?"

She shrugged one shoulder. "I got dressed, fed and sheltered. She made sure of that."

He noticed what was missing. "Did she care for you in other ways, too? Basic necessities are good, but not enough for the soul."

"The soul?" She repeated the words without looking up. "She took care of me the best she could."

But not emotionally, he suspected. She wouldn't have had much energy left over for that from the sound of it.

Then her head popped up. "Are you saying I'm emotionally crippled?"

At that point, he figured he should have kept his mouth shut. None of his business, no training to help him, and he might just have stirred up a hornet's nest. How could he respond to that? He hadn't exactly been suggesting that, but...but what? Getting too nosy for his own good? Then she surprised him.

"If so," she said, "you'd be right. I've been thinking about it lately. I've never really had a truly close relationship. I wouldn't know what to do with one. Maybe I was built this way, or maybe something inside me is frozen, but..." Again she hesitated. "I guess I always live in anticipation of having to move again. Leave everything behind. It's the way I've been ever since I can remember. I can't blame anyone for it, Tim. This is just how I am."

He decided he needed to let her off the hook he might

have put her on. "I'm sure lots of other people feel the same. It doesn't mean something is wrong with you."

"Maybe not. On the other hand…" She shook her head and once again studied the coffee she wasn't drinking. "I *do* wonder what it would have been like to grow up in one place, with lifelong friends. Would I have been different?"

She might well have been, he thought. But that was water over the dam now. The question was only if she was happy with herself and her life the way it was. He wasn't going to ask that question, because he didn't have the right.

He also had no comparison. He'd been firmly planted here his entire life. He knew damn near everyone, knew who could be trusted, who couldn't, whom he liked to spend time with and those he preferred to avoid. He knew almost every inch of his world intimately. Vanessa couldn't say that. In fact, from the sound of it, she avoided it.

"You know," she said after a bit, "I don't even date. Not really. Or maybe I should rephrase that. I've dated a few times, but not for long. Once things start to pass light friendship, I always bail. So am I crippled? I guess so. Other than your marriage, have you had other relationships?"

"Nothing enduring," he admitted. "I'd be the first to say that Claire's death made me reluctant to hang myself out there for another blow."

She nodded, her gaze meeting his at last. "That's how I feel most of the time. I think. I'm still trying to figure it out. I just know that I feel as if I'm standing back all the time. Staying on the outside. It's safe."

It would have been easy to answer with a flippant *whatever works for you*, but he didn't. Some instinct warned him that would be exactly the wrong thing to say, because right now something about her felt vulnerable to him. As if some of those walls had lowered just a bit. He didn't know if that was good or bad, but it was best left alone—by him, at least.

Damn, he couldn't remember ever feeling so uncertain in his dealings with another person.

He sat in perplexity, wondering why it even mattered to him. Nice enough lady. Too sexually attractive for his comfort. But she was leaving in a week or two for Albuquerque, and their contacts afterward would probably consist of email or phone calls discussing his progress in readying the house for sale.

Just treat her like any other customer, he warned himself. Because that's all she was. Any of her problems aside from the house were none of his business.

Tim wasn't the only troubled person at that table. This trip had awakened things in Vanessa, or maybe it had acted as a major revelation. Maybe she *was* closed off because of her childhood. She'd never really considered it before, because lots of people moved often when they were children. Much of this country had been on the move one way or another since the Second World War. Other people seemed fine, despite bouncing around.

But the definition of *fine* was what she was suddenly calling into question. Of course she was fine. She had a productive career that she loved. She had pursuits that she enjoyed. She just didn't let anyone get too close, and that didn't seem to bother most people.

Honestly, she didn't think most people wanted to know her too well. Or anyone else, for that matter. Skimming along the surface kept things from getting messy for everyone.

But maybe that wasn't working for her anymore. Why else was she questioning herself?

When Matthew went upstairs to get ready for bed, Tim went with him. She could hear the two of them laughing, water running in the tub. Normal sounds she hadn't heard in a very long time because she'd been an only child. Something about them made her ache.

Made her ache for things she'd told herself she never wanted and didn't need. Look at her parents. Who'd want to get married? Look at herself. She had no idea how to be a good parent. Tim might make it look easy, but she knew perfectly well how many mistakes could be made. And marrying someone meant letting them inside places she'd been guarding ever since she could remember, places where she could be wounded.

Why had she never taken a really hard look at this before? Why had she never begun to imagine that she might be warped by the way she had grown up? Just because nobody else seemed to notice anything was wrong?

Like tonight. She'd felt Tim pull back time and again as if he feared her response. He'd edged close to very personal things but had tried to be reassuring. Or had chosen silence.

Maybe he was just being respectful. Or maybe he sensed she wasn't quite right.

God, she needed to take a really hard look at herself and decide if she wanted to stay on her present path. Because the sound of Matthew's laughter upstairs really made her wonder.

Chapter Seven

"Tomorrow's a day off," Tim announced as he returned. "Shall we go into the living room? Bring your coffee if you want."

She left her coffee behind and went to sit on the couch with him. "Why tomorrow off?"

"Sunday. Today was long enough, and I happen to know for a fact that Matthew hasn't even started his homework. So I'll take him to the early church service tomorrow then bring him back to study. He always has more homework on weekends."

She nodded, trying to remember how much homework she'd had at that age. Not much, if she remembered correctly.

"Want to come to church with us?"

Everything inside her froze. See all those people? "No. Thanks," she added.

"I didn't think so. Anyway, Matthew likes the kids' service. And I don't mind catching up with people I only get to see on weekends. Surprising how many there are. The working life," he added on a chuckle. "I'll bring home something for breakfast. Then… Monday. Once we get the air in that house tested, we might be able to get to work. When you said gut it, how much do you want to gut?"

Vanessa, however, was still hung up at her reaction to going to church with him. She went to church nearly every Sunday at home, so her reaction had to do with this being Conard County. Her father's fears and hatreds riding her hard and strong.

She wished she had the courage to just go, but then couldn't see any reason. Face the demons she'd never have to face again? It seemed like a waste of energy.

"Gutting the house?" Tim prompted gently.

"Oh. Yeah. I don't know. I mean, I guess what I want to do is erase Bob. Paint, wallpaper. I don't think I was talking about tearing out walls or anything."

Still smiling, he nodded. "Got it. We can get the last of the furnishings out of there after the inspector comes. He said around ten o'clock."

"Okay." So much easier to talk about the house than going to church. Now wasn't that weird?

"I hope we get good news," Tim remarked. "The house isn't *that* old. There might not be any lead at all. Although I had to remodel a house that had asbestos in the joint compound used on the drywall. Safe as long as it was coated with paint, but the family didn't want it anyway. Removing it required hiring some skilled people who have all the protective gear. Just to be safe."

"Are you trying to scare me?" she asked, looking at him from the corner of her eye.

He laughed. "Absolutely not. I'm expecting to be pleasantly surprised on Monday."

"I hope you're right."

"I usually am." He winked. "I've remodeled a lot of houses around here. Very few problems, even on the older ones. It's been a long time since people became aware of the dangers of lead and so on. Many took care of it before I came along. And like I said, if it's sealed under paint, no real problem."

"But we have sagging paint," she reminded him.

"And we'll deal with it."

He seemed so sure of himself. The way she did in her lab at the museum, only he was confident in so many other ways. He knew his job, of course, but he also seemed comfortable in dealing with his son.

Today as she'd watched him work with all the people who traipsed through the house, showing them things, sometimes helping them carry out heavier items, he'd been so comfortable. Meanwhile, she'd sat at the kitchen table like a slightly nervous mouse.

Man, was that who she really was? A mouse? Timid?

But maybe it was just the situation. At home she didn't feel timid. She just didn't link up with other people a whole lot. An introvert. Nothing wrong with that.

Or maybe there was. She'd been completely thrown out of her comfort zone by coming to a place she'd been taught to think of as bad. Only it wasn't bad. Except for that crazy visit from Larry, everyone had been pleasant, and to judge by the people at the sale today, it seemed most had forgotten the past. Maybe she was being jarred by the difference between reality and expectation.

She spoke again. "I guess I need to reevaluate."

"What?"

"My opinion of Conard County."

"Maybe so. At this point Larry is the only person you met who lived down to your father's expectations."

She nodded. "It's true."

"But honestly, Vannie, I'm not sure the situation was as bad, as regards other people here, as your father thought. He got conned, too. I think most people around here were able to figure that out."

"Maybe. But I'm not going to take a poll. So far, with the exception of Larry, everyone's been nice."

"And don't forget that Ashley wants you to come talk to her class. You'll wind up being the famous dinosaur lady around here if you do."

"A much better way to be remembered," she agreed, smiling almost in spite of herself. "If I'm going to do that, I should call the museum on Monday and have them express me some materials to use. Graphics and models would be a whole lot more fun for kids than me just standing there talking and drawing on a chalkboard."

"Ah, we've evolved to whiteboards."

A small laugh escaped her. "But still. I should also get them to send some puzzles for Matthew. It's an awfully long time for him to wait for me to send them after I go home."

"So you're staying longer?"

Something in the way he asked it caused her breath to lock in her throat. Almost timidly, she looked at him.

"You're beautiful," he said, his voice just above a whisper. "So beautiful, Vannie. Do you even realize it?"

She shook her head once, stiffly, wishing she could draw a full breath.

He scooted down the couch until he sat right beside her. "I'm going to kiss you," he murmured. "You've got exactly one chance to say no."

She couldn't have said that word if her life had depended on it. It had been a long time since anyone had kissed her, and a full lifetime since she'd been as attracted to a man as she was to Tim. There could be no harm in this. Just a kiss.

"I shouldn't," he whispered just before his mouth settled on hers.

It was the gentlest of touches, as if he expected rejection and wanted to leave room for it. Light as butterfly wings, but the warmth it sent spiraling through her amazed her. Then his work-hardened hand cupped her cheek and he deepened the kiss, running his tongue along her lips until her head tipped back a little and she granted him entry.

As his tongue slipped into her mouth and swirled gently, she felt herself softening in every cell of her body, becoming pliable, hungering for more.

She was melting, an experience she'd never had before. How could feelings so strong make her feel so soft?

She wanted his arms around her, wanted to feel his strength, but just as she was lifting her own hand to encourage him, he drew back a little to sprinkle kisses on her eyelids and her cheeks.

"To be continued," he said huskily, then pulled away, placing distance between them.

To be continued? She didn't even want to open her

eyes, never wanted to lose the soft feeling that filled her, or the gentle but electric desire that had come with it.

Just one kiss…

In an instant, near panic filled her. What was she doing? If ever there was a way to get hurt, this was it. She wouldn't just be able to walk away and laugh it off. She knew how hard she could take things. Look at her whole life.

Jumping up, she uttered a smothered good-night and headed for the bedroom.

Some risks were too great. She needed to change a whole lot to be willing to take this one.

Yeah, she was emotionally crippled.

But she was also safe.

Tim didn't move. What had possessed him? Something in the way she looked at him, but whatever he thought he'd seen hadn't been there. So he'd kissed her, sent her into flight and made a total hash of something that had been perfectly fine until he acted like an idiot.

Closing his eyes, he reviewed what had happened. He'd been so sure she was reaching out to him. Asking for a taste, just a taste, of what it would be like if she crossed her barriers.

Just a little kiss, nothing more. Nothing that should have caused her to flee. While it had caused his blood to pound, she usually made that happen just by being around. He doubted she'd reacted as strongly with desire.

He'd felt, just briefly, the softening in her as if she wanted to yield, though. In the process he'd evidently pushed her past her defenses. Because he was damn sure he hadn't repelled her.

The expression on her face when he had backed away had been so soft, so blissful. He wished she could look that way all the time. Then something had hit her, and she'd jumped like a rabbit with a hawk after it.

Well, he'd done it. He'd sent her into protective flight, even though he'd pulled back quickly and said only, "To be continued." He hadn't forced himself on her, and he'd made it clear nothing more would happen between them right then.

But her flight had given him a measure of the scars she bore. The fears she tried to conceal but that buried her in isolation. Could moving around that much as a child really make someone so afraid of getting close, of potential loss? Or had there been more?

He of course had no idea. How could he? Worse, he'd upset her, and he didn't know how to fix it. Judging by the way she'd taken off, she'd probably start talking about moving to the motel.

He didn't like that idea. For her sake, mostly, but also for his.

All he'd wanted to do was help this woman get through what was plainly a rough time for her. Earl had told him maybe more than he should have, being her lawyer, about her reluctance to even come back here, and her distaste for that house.

But instead of helping Vanessa, he might have just made everything more difficult for her. Didn't that just take the cake?

In the bedroom, Vanessa sat in the padded Boston rocker that was tucked into a corner and calmed herself down. When the near panic ebbed enough that rational thought took control, she loathed herself.

How could she have reacted that way? It was over the top. So a man had kissed her then let her go. Just a freaking kiss. She hated to think how her reaction must have made him feel. She was afraid of rejection, but she'd just given Tim one of the worst types of rejections of all time.

She needed to apologize but didn't know how. What was more, she didn't think she should offer an apology before she got herself sorted out. She had to find a way to explain herself to him…and to herself.

The extremity of her reaction frightened her in and of itself. Was she truly that far gone? It was one thing to keep her emotions locked up and observe a safe but polite distance from others. Nobody seemed to have a problem with that. As she'd noticed before, nobody seemed to notice, either. While she knew people who'd pour their hearts out to her, she never reciprocated and they never seemed to detect the absence.

So her guardedness served her well enough most of the time. But not this time. This time Tim had expressed desire for her, and she'd fled as if he were a demon. That was awful.

In fact, she'd done the very thing to him that she was so afraid of. Despicable behavior. Shame filled her.

Of course, Tim might be able to handle it better than she could have, but that still didn't relieve her of responsibility to apologize for her flight.

Closing her eyes, she thought of the many nice and helpful things he'd done for her in her short time here, and knew she owed him some truly straight answers.

She'd already let him know that she didn't get close to people. She'd talked with him about something she never mentioned: her lousy childhood. But it was wrong to expect him to put it together and manufacture her excuses for her.

At last, rising, she marched out to the living room, hoping he hadn't gone upstairs. Whatever kind of mea culpa she could manage, he deserved it.

He was still sitting on the couch. He must have heard her coming, because he was looking toward the entry-way.

"You okay?" he asked before she could speak a word.

"I'm fine." As fine as she knew how to be, except for scalding shame. "I'm so sorry that—"

He cut her off. "No apology needed. If you aren't scared to death of me now, come join me."

"Scared to death of you?" That's what she had made him think. Oh, God, she was an awful person. But she had run like a frightened deer. Not so much because she was scared of him, but because she was terrified of herself.

Somehow she needed to explain that. Sitting down gingerly on the couch, a foot away from him, she cleared her throat. Once again, before she could say anything, he spoke.

"I'm sorry I upset you, Vannie. That wasn't my intent."

No, she thought. That hadn't been his intent at all. He'd given her a gentle kiss, almost a testing, questing kiss, giving her ample opportunity to respond or pull away. Instead, she had run.

"I'm the one who is sorry," she said. "My reaction was out of all proportion."

He studied her, turning sideways on the couch, pulling up one bent leg and resting his arm along the back. "Wanna talk?"

She, who never talked about her real feelings, understood she would have to do it now. At least a little, because he deserved it. But it wasn't going to be easy, because it meant exposing parts of herself she didn't even like to review in the privacy of her own mind.

"I told you I was crippled. That was just a part of it that you saw. You got close to me, emotionally, and I reacted badly without thinking. For that I owe you an apology. You didn't demand anything of me. I could have just let the moment slip by. Instead, like a freak, I ran."

"You're no freak," he said quietly. "Look, you gave me only a sketch of what your childhood was like, but I'm not surprised from even that little you shared that you've got some pretty sturdy walls around yourself. Losing everything at an early age, a dropout alcoholic father who kept you moving all the time you were growing up... Just that makes it unsurprising that you don't want a close connection. I know what it feels like when somebody you really care about is ripped out of your life."

Yes, he certainly understood that. "But all you did was kiss me."

To her surprise, he smiled. "A kiss can be a gateway drug."

After a moment, in spite of herself, she had to smile back.

"Sometimes," he said. "Sometimes it's enough to

make folks take an instant cure. Either way, it's a big deal, and it was pulling you places you clearly don't want to go. I get it, and I don't blame you."

"You're awfully understanding."

"Maybe. I don't know. I've got my own hang-ups. I'm widowed. I've got a kid I've got to think about every time I make a decision. Losing Claire left a hole in me that will always be there, so I get that part. It took me a while to realize that I was just going to have to learn to live with it, because they don't make a patch to cover grief. And for a while I was sparing of my emotions. That wasn't good for Matthew. Even I could figure that one out. Thank God I did before I created permanent damage."

"All I see when I look at the two of you is that you're a good father." Then a snort escaped her. "As if I'm any judge of that."

He tilted his head a bit. "I think you'd be the best judge of a bad father."

She closed her eyes a moment, allowing tension to begin to seep away. He was making this so easy for her. He made her feel as if she could safely tell him anything.

But that was the real danger, wasn't it? Opening herself up, then getting kicked one way or another. There was certainly no point in opening up to Tim. She was leaving. She'd lose him, too.

But then an odd little notion prickled at her. It would be different, because she'd be leaving by choice. She wouldn't be dragged away against her will. So maybe he was safe to open up to because she was in control of the limits.

Then she felt shame again. She couldn't treat him that way. Invite him in, then toss him when she left. What if he developed feelings? Although why he should she couldn't imagine.

"Look," he said. "Let's just let it lie. No apology necessary. Your reaction was honest, and I understand it. No need for any soul baring on your part. Life leaves its marks on us all. We deal with them as best we can."

"But am I dealing?"

He placed his hand lightly on her shoulder. "As best you can."

He rose. "Come on, help me make some coffee cake. Matthew loves it when we have it on Sunday morning. Let's make him grin."

Making Matthew grin was always a worthy enterprise. Summoning a smile, she followed him.

Tim had several different recipes he used for coffee cake, but he chose one he could have prepared blindfolded because his mind was busy buzzing around the things Vanessa had said.

It had taken guts for her to come apologize for her behavior and to try to explain. For a woman who claimed she wanted no close connections, she nonetheless acted like one who actually cared about how others felt.

He measured cinnamon and brown sugar into a bowl with butter and asked if she'd mind crumbling it with the pastry cutter. "Matthew loves crumb toppings."

"Who wouldn't?" she responded.

The cake he was making wouldn't be very sweet, but it would be full of blueberries. His nod to being conscious of what his son ate. Ha.

With the oven preheating, he got to work making the cake.

"So this is a special occasion thing? The coffee cake?"

"Yeah. Easy enough to make, but they might take away my parenting license if I did it too often. And if I did it too often, it wouldn't be special anymore."

"Good point."

"Have you decided if you want to talk to Ashley's class?"

"I'm going to ask the museum to express materials to make it more interesting. Did I tell you that or just think it?"

"Darned if I know at this point." He laughed. "Sometimes my head gets crowded and some stuff slips out the holes in it."

She laughed. "Is that what you tell Matthew?"

"Often enough. Honestly, I get preoccupied and forget things. He's used to it. Sometimes he even works at being my memory, especially when it's about important matters. Important to him, anyway."

"I haven't noticed you having any memory problems."

"You haven't known me that long. I can get deeply absorbed in thinking about a project and I become absentminded. Trust me, Matthew never forgets a thing."

"I can just imagine. I bet it could be dangerous to make him a promise."

He winked at her over his shoulder, then went back to stirring the batter. "I never make promises. Too many things can happen. It frustrates him sometimes when I say only that I'll try. I get plenty of reminders, though."

After he oiled the square glass baking dish, he poured the batter into it. The crumb topping was ready, and he spread it over the top. "Everyone likes this," he remarked. "I hope you will, too."

"I'm sure I will. I'm with Matthew on crumb toppings."

But then the cake was in the oven and there seemed to be no more casual conversation. Forty minutes before the cake would be done, and here he was feeling awkward. It was a rare feeling for him, probably arising from the way he'd upset her earlier, and then the conversation between them that had threatened to become intense.

It had certainly been revealing, but he wasn't sure either of them wanted the intensity they'd been approaching. He doubted that, despite her self-questioning and self-criticism, Vanessa really wanted to let fly with her emotions. She was skimming her own problems in the way she seemed to want to skim most things. Touch on them, but don't really mine them.

He had to admit that might be the best thing unless she was talking to a shrink. She could recognize her scars without tearing them open. Name them, so he'd understand, but not root around in them.

What was wrong with that? But it reminded him to tread carefully. And that made him uncertain about what direction to take. He generally wasn't the type to resort to conversations about the weather unless some big event was on the way.

"The snowman is almost gone," she remarked. "He's looking sad. I guess the sun is doing that?"

"That would be my guess," he answered, relieved. "It sure hasn't gotten above freezing since the storm."

"I really enjoyed doing that." She smiled and finally looked at him with a relaxed smile, her eyes clear of shadows. "I'd given up hope." A little laugh escaped her. "I never thought I'd be part of building one that looks so classic."

"More hands to build it, maybe," he suggested. "It looks like it should be easy, but it's not, really." A click from the coffeepot reminded him it was still on. "Do you want more coffee or should I turn the pot off?"

"I'm done, thanks. There's a hope that I can sleep tonight."

That caught his attention. "Do you have problems sleeping?"

"Occasionally. Doesn't everyone?"

"I never do," he confessed. "Probably because I don't hold still very much. Always working or riding herd on a kid who operates at ninety miles an hour."

That drew a comfortable laugh from her. "He never slows down," she agreed. "He even plays video games at top speed. Boy, did he make me feel slow. He's clicking those buttons as easily as moving his fingers, and I'm fumbling around. You'd never guess the delicacy of some of my work." She shrugged. "Of course, I have no practice."

"That might be key," he remarked, at last pulling out a chair and sitting across the table from her. "He's been playing that game for several years."

"You don't have a problem with it?"

He shook his head. "Why would I? He's not living in the basement 24/7. He gets out to play, he's doing well in school. Now if that was *all* he did..."

"Yeah. I don't get why some people think it's a bad

influence. Kids can develop some real skills, and the latest studies show that even kids who play violent games become less violent than those who play none at all. Surprisingly enough. Of course, are these things really ever settled?"

"I wouldn't know, it's not my field." Relieved that she was talking, he let her run. "I just know that I don't let him play anything that isn't PG. I'm glad the boxes have ratings, because his last two birthdays and Christmas he wanted new games and I was able to check out their suitability without having to play them myself."

She nodded. "The one I played with him required a lot of problem solving. I was impressed."

"There you go."

"My dinosaurs are going to pale in comparison."

"I doubt it."

"I don't." Her smile widened. "Over the last few decades, we've had to put in a lot of interactive exhibits, moving exhibits. Kids aren't content to just walk through a museum and look through glass."

The last of the earlier tension was leaving him as well. He relaxed back into his chair, considering whether to get a beer, then deciding against it. She was so pretty when her face was unclouded, so happy-looking when she talked about her job. Just leave her be, he warned himself. No more kissing. No more giving in to the desire that kept riding him. He had no right to upset her balance, a balance he suspected had been hard to achieve.

"Do you think it's bad that you've had to put in all those interactive exhibits?" he asked.

"Absolutely not. When I escape my lab, I love watching the schoolkids come through. They get so excited and intrigued. I hope they carry that away with them."

"They're the important ones," he replied. "You know, when I was about twelve, my parents took me on a trip to DC. One of the most memorable stops for me was at the Smithsonian. But a funny story. My dad could get lost in artifacts for hours, but my mother was having none of it. She told him that while he might enjoy looking at brass buttons, I wouldn't, so we needed to go look at more exciting things. We went off to the Air and Space Museum, which was a blast, but somehow she squeezed in a look at the inaugural gowns of the first ladies."

Vanessa laughed. "I guess she wasn't interested in those buttons, either."

"That was my read." He grinned. "My dad was a contractor, too, but also a history buff. A man made for museums."

"I love museums," she said. "Everything about them. Some day I'd love to get to the antiquities museum in Cairo, and the Louvre in Paris. Just for starters. If I added any more to my list, I'd probably lose hope of doing any of it."

"The Smithsonian's easier to get to."

"Cheaper, for sure," she said. "I've been there a couple of times, and I'll go back. But right now we're working on making our museum one of the best places to go in Albuquerque. Of course, we're competing with the Museum of Natural History and Science. I think we have enough bridge topics to help us grow, though. And our research departments cooperate as much as possible, and we exchange temporary exhibits. You can't have too much science."

He enjoyed watching her climb on her hobby horse. It was a different side of her, a lively, assured and confident side, so different from most of what he'd seen of her. "So you're involved in building a new museum?"

"It's not new. We're just growing it. So far, so good."

"But the research is your thing."

"Very much so." She closed her eyes, still smiling. "I can get lost in my lab, forget the time, the day. Mysteries, puzzles—always something new to think about."

Well, she surely wouldn't find that here, he thought, wondering why the idea saddened him. From the start he'd known she was going home, that she had a career there. Why should that bother him now?

Maybe he needed to take a page from her book and avoid getting involved. He glanced at the clock. Still twenty minutes on the cake.

"I must be boring you," she said.

"Not at all." He really wasn't bored. Too many of his thoughts were selfish right now. Thoughts like he wished he had more time to get to know her, that she'd stay here longer than a week or two, that she wasn't so skittish, because for the first time since Claire he was ready to dive into a relationship, with Vanessa. She'd awakened a part of him he had begun to think was dead forever.

He wanted a woman again. He wanted to make her laugh, bring her a rose and do all that sappy stuff. Oh, man, he was headed for trouble, and he didn't know how to stop it. This train had left the station.

So he thought about Matthew. He needed to protect his son, and since Matthew seemed to really like

Vanessa, he needed to be careful that the boy didn't start hoping she'd be a permanent fixture.

He stifled a sigh, wondering how his mostly smooth life had suddenly become as roiled as a river during spring flooding. Unwanted thoughts and needs were messing everything up, and it was a losing situation. The only thing he stood to gain from this was creating another crater in his life. Not fair to Matthew.

Think with the big head, he told himself with some humor.

Then Vanessa proved she had more gumption than he thought. She shocked him by asking, "Could we try that kiss again sometime?"

His head spun. What the hell? She'd fled. But maybe knowing she had to go home made her feel safer. To hell with that, he thought, as a burst of anger hit him. "I'm not a science experiment," he said shortly.

"No, you're not. I didn't mean…" She trailed off, then eventually said, "I'm sorry, Tim. Good night."

He watched her leave, and for long moments didn't care that she was gone. Try it again? Why? So she could go home and not fear being kissed again? Screw that.

But as his anger ebbed, he sat alone in his kitchen, suddenly feeling lonely, and wondering if he'd misinterpreted her intention.

No, probably not, he reassured himself. After all, she *had* run away. If she was getting ready to try her wings, then she ought to try them with some man back home.

Not with him. God, why had he ever kissed her in the first place?

Glumly he regarded his own behavior and wondered about himself.

Chapter Eight

"How do we get this off?" Vanessa asked on Tuesday, her voice startling Tim.

Sunday had passed quietly. Vanessa and Tim seemed to have reached a silent agreement to maintain a mutual distance. Vanessa played video games with Matthew and joined him while he did his homework. Matthew's bubbling conversation was all that kept dinner from being utterly quiet.

Monday the inspector arrived and after a number of hours gave them good news. The air was fine, and if there was any lead in the house, he couldn't find it. There was some asbestos in the corners of rooms where drywall had been taped, so it was probably in all the drywall mud, but nothing to worry about as long as it was painted. They got the go-ahead for renovations, the only warning being to wear protective masks if they decided to pull down drywall.

Tim could live with that. But now Vanessa was staring at sagging paint in one of the bedrooms, and she'd been quiet for so long he'd almost forgotten she was in the house.

This version wasn't going well, either, he thought. Bad when they'd danced too close, possibly worse now that they were dancing away. Dang, he wished they could find a decent middle ground. He seemed to have ruined that by kissing her.

He came to stand beside her, eyeing the wall. "Latex paint can be cool."

"Meaning?"

"It's full of latex. A lot of that will come off in sheets." To show her, he pulled one edge, and the paint didn't resist. Down it came, all in one sheet, leaving little patches behind here and there. When it was done, it looked like he was holding a huge piece of Swiss cheese.

Vanessa surprised him by laughing. "I didn't know it could do that."

"Age and exposure to temperature changes helped us here. Don't try this at home." Her laugh pleased him, and he hoped she was loosening up a little.

But not every wall boasted sagging paint. He'd need to check it to make sure it was adhering well enough to paint over. Then there was the wallpaper. The paste had begun to dry into dust, pieces had left the wall, corners were falling down, but there was still a lot that would need heat to release it.

"I hate removing wallpaper," he remarked. "Tedious. But this stuff has to go, so we're going to do a lot of steaming and scraping. You'll be glad to know I have a couple of guys to help, so you won't be stuck with too much work."

She looked at him. "You never mentioned employees."

"Ah, but I have them. If this were my own place, I could take my sweet time. Customers wouldn't like that too much, so yes, I have help. The guys have been working on another job, but they're just about done, so we should see them soon. We'll make quick work of this for you."

"I don't mind helping."

"I didn't say you couldn't help," he reminded her. "Just that the two of us aren't going to try to complete this job before you have to leave. Plus, I'm sure you want to get this place off your back as quickly as possible." He returned to his examination of the wallpaper.

Well, that had certainly been her intention when she arrived here, Vanessa thought. Find the quickest way to dump this house and put this unwanted piece of the past completely behind her.

Oddly, now that she'd been in here so many times, and was now helping to change the entire space, she didn't feel the same hatred toward it. She was getting used to it.

So while it wasn't weighing on her the way it had been, and her desire to be done with it quickly was fading, she felt the wall growing slowly between her and Tim.

Worse, she knew whose fault that was: hers. She was

the builder of walls, and he was merely respecting what he sensed from her.

She left the room without saying anything, needing a few minutes by herself. She'd been afraid of coming back here, but apparently for all the wrong reasons. Except for Larry—and what was with him, anyway?— the people she'd met had been kind and friendly. They didn't hold her responsible for something that had happened when she was a child. Amazing that she had ever thought they would.

The fact that her father's fears had become so deeply embedded required her to look into her heart and mind and find the rest of the mistaken thinking she might have soaked up.

Her response to Tim was a great example. She was drawn to him as she'd never been drawn before. He awoke sexual feelings in her that she'd buried years ago out of fear. Why not let them blossom? Why was she shoving him away?

Regardless of the desire she felt, she had to admit he'd been a cheerful, friendly guy when she arrived, welcoming her into his home so she wouldn't have to sleep alone in the nightmare house or at the miserable motel. His son had already won a place in her heart.

So here she was giving that wonderful man a good look at her moat. That wasn't nice. At the very least, considering all that he was doing for her, she needed to be friendly. Not distant.

What's more, she wasn't only disturbed by her cool behavior to a man so helpful. She was disturbed that he seemed to want her to be gone quickly. Now she wasn't the one in a rush—he seemed to be. Of course, he attributed that to her own expressed desire, but she didn't quite believe that.

No, she had offended him. She'd just about hit him in the face with her weirdness. Why wouldn't he want her gone as quickly as possible? She was living in his house, making friends with his son and treating him coolly, if not rudely.

Man, she was messed up. And when she'd tried to reach past her barriers and suggest another kiss at some future date, of course he hadn't leaped at the chance. She could understand his behavior after her reaction, but what the heck was *she* thinking?

She'd gone from a self-contained professional into a dithering jerk in an instant. The path was clear. Avoid entanglement and go home. So why did she keep chasing that around in her head? Why couldn't she settle? One way or another, make up her mind about what she was doing here and what she wanted to do. Become again the person who had arrived here with very clear goals.

"I'm getting very tired of myself," she said aloud. She stood in the empty living room by herself, and faced the fact that everything inside her had somehow gotten very mixed-up in less than a week. But being unable to make decisions wasn't like her. Wandering around thinking the same thoughts over and over wasn't like her.

"There you are," she heard Tim say behind her. "I thought I heard you say something."

"Talking to myself." Slowly she faced him. Then she blurted something she shouldn't have. A thought that emerged only as it passed her lips. "You've messed up my head."

He froze, then put his hands on his narrow hips. "And just how the hell did I do that?"

Good question, she thought, horrified that she'd spoken such a thing. *He* wasn't responsible. She was. "Sorry. I'm responsible for my own mess."

He released a breath. "You know, it was never my intention to mess you up. But if you ask me, you were already messed up when you got here. A nicely organized mess, but still a mess. That's not blaming you, by the way. I heard enough from you to guess you were seriously hammered by your youth. We all live with the leftovers from that, and you have more bad than many. So what the hell is pushing you over the edge, Vanessa? You can pack up and go home right now if that'll make you feel better. I can finish out this job now that I know what you want. I just thought you might feel better by doing a little destruction on Bob's house. Maybe not. Your dinosaur bones are waiting."

He turned and took a step away before she called out his name. He stopped but kept his back to her.

"Tim... I'm sorry. I'm not blaming you, and I shouldn't have made it sound like I was. Coming here has rattled me. *You* rattle me. But that doesn't mean I should inflict the fallout on you. I need to get my head straight. I need to sort some things out. Just ignore me. It's my problem. Things I haven't realized, things I haven't faced—they all seem to be coming to a head. I need some counseling, but that's not your job."

"No, and I wouldn't know where to begin." He turned and looked at her again. "Let's just rip this place up. Take out your frustration and confusion on this house. God knows it could benefit from it."

Then he walked away, teaching her in an instant that she still knew how to feel lonely.

Yup, she was a mess.

Wednesday afternoon, the express package she'd requested arrived from the museum. Matthew watched eagerly as she opened it, but the first thing she noticed was the condition of her hands. Nicked, raw knuckles, three bandages...they hadn't looked this bad since she'd been digging up the fossils. The thought made her smile as she cut the tape with a box cutter Tim had given her to use. He, too, watched but from a greater distance. Matthew was practically on top of her.

After she removed the padding from the huge box, she began to remove items. "Posters," she said, reading the labels on three cardboard tubes. "Great, I can leave these for the classroom."

"Can you open them now?" Matthew asked.

"After I check the other stuff, okay?"

He settled back, watching.

An envelope contained stacks of several kinds of colorful pamphlets suitable to the age group. Then a bigger box that revealed three larger dinosaur models that someone must have cannibalized from individual boxes on sale in the gift shop. The kids could handle them and pass them around. Another box was clearly labeled—it contained a skeletal model of the T. rex, everyone's favorite. The students would absolutely love that.

And finally, at the bottom, were the two boxes she'd wanted for Matthew.

"These are for you," she told him. "One is a triceratops, and the other is a T. rex. They're wood puzzles so you can build the skeletons."

He took the boxes one after the other, studying the pictures on the front and repeatedly murmuring, "Thank you. Wow, oh, wow." Then he looked up at his dad. "Can I open them and start?"

"Homework?" Tim asked.

Matthew's face fell. He rose from the floor then hugged the boxes to his chest. They were almost too big for him to hold both at the same time. "After homework," he agreed.

"And don't rush it," Tim said. "I'm going to check it over. Then we can open your presents and see what's in there."

"He's amazing," Vanessa said, watching him walk toward the dining room. "Not many kids would have even asked." Not that she had all that much experience.

"We all have to learn about delayed gratification sooner or later," he answered. "Would I like to let him open them now? Of course. But then he'd never get to his homework. And I want to thank you, Vannie. Those are a really great gift."

"I hope he gets a kick out of them. And I guess I should call Ashley and ask her when she wants me to come in."

He leaned against the doorjamb, folding his arms and crossing his legs loosely at the ankle. "So you've decided to do that?"

She nodded as she began to replace items in the box. "Kids go nuts for this stuff. I've given talks like this before. Why deprive Ashley's class just because of where I am?"

"Still have bad feelings about this town?"

She gave a small shake of her head. "Not as much, but I have to admit I'm kind of looking out for Larry. Which is silly, I guess. He had his say. What more is there?"

"Well, if he tries to say any more, I'll be nearby. The guy has at least one small screw loose, to judge by that display. But I wouldn't worry about it, Vannie."

"I'm not, really. Just occasionally uneasy. I'm not used to people shouting in my face these days."

He paused then asked, "Did they used to?"

"My dad, of course. He was the last one."

"I hope the only one, although that's bad enough."

She shrugged one shoulder as she placed the poster tubes back in the box. "I didn't like it at all, but I'm still here." Then she tossed him a smile. "I have to admit I can hardly wait to see Matthew open those boxes. I hope he'll enjoy 3-D puzzles."

"He still plays with Legos, and he has a big bucket of them. Is this different?"

"It doesn't fit together as easily. It also includes a washable glue for putting the pieces permanently into place. But I recommend he put them together once before gluing."

Tim laughed. "Amen to that. Like, measure twice, cut once. A good practice with most things." He straightened. "I need to get that chicken ready for roasting. Oh, and Ashley's number is ASHLEY G."

"Seriously? How'd she do that?"

"Not on purpose. She laughed about it for years, but someone else pointed it out to her. She'd never noticed."

"I can see why. I hate having to dial letters."

"I run into trouble because the numbers are backward on the telephone from what they are on an adding machine or on my computer keypad. I still wonder why they did that."

"Because most people weren't using adding machines?"

He laughed. "Maybe so. Off to the kitchen."

Vanessa's first call was to Glenn at the museum to thank him for pulling together that wonderful box so fast.

"Hey, I'm all about education," he reminded her. Given that he was in charge of the museum's educational programs, there was no arguing with that.

Vanessa laughed. "True that. But I really appreciate it. I didn't think you could get it here so fast."

"Like I had to dig that stuff out of an ancient burial mound? Come on, you know we have stacks of it. It only took me a few minutes to pull together what you asked for. Still planning on going skiing?"

She hesitated. "No," she answered finally. "I'm working on the house with the contractor. It's kind of cathartic."

Glenn knew only snatches of her story, but he seemed understand her meaning. "Go for it. Sometimes I wish I had something to demolish."

After Glenn, she called Ashley, who sounded delighted to hear from her.

"You've been gone so long," Ashley said. "But you know, I think of you from time to time and I wondered where you'd gone. We used to be thick as thieves. So... any chance you could find time for lunch while you're here? I could ask Julie to join us if her husband can watch the baby."

Baby? For some reason the idea took Vanessa aback. Julie had a baby? Wow, some time had surely passed. Still, she hesitated. "I was just calling to tell you I got the materials to do a presentation for your class."

Ashley paused noticeably, and her tone changed slightly. "That's super. When do you want to do it? Just let me know."

Vanessa almost laughed. "You're the teacher with the lesson plan. I thought you'd tell me."

"Friday, then? In the afternoon, say, one? Because we'll be done with the necessary lessons and you'd be just what I need to settle them down a bit—they'll be getting antsy for the end of the day and the weekend."

"That's perfect," Vanessa agreed. "I'll be there."

Then Ashley said one more time, "Lunch on Saturday? I'd love to catch up."

Vanessa felt once again her own internal resistance to relationships, to this town, to all the bugaboos of her childhood. This time, however, her spine stiffened. "I'd enjoy that. What time and where?"

Oh, God, she thought as she hung up. A public diner. How many other Larrys might there be out there? Unless she could get ill before then, it appeared she was going to find out.

Tim proved to be as interested in the puzzles as Matthew. They opened them after dinner in the dining room, and Matthew went over the first sheet of directions carefully, asking for help when he didn't understand something. Tim did the answering. Vanessa would have gladly jumped in but restrained herself. She knew those models inside and out. Matthew—and Tim, apparently—was delighting in a journey of discovery.

Then came a large piece of flannel-backed oilcloth for Matthew to work on.

Tim showed Matthew how to match all the puzzle pieces to the list of parts, then sat back and let him make sure they were all there.

A builder instructing his son. Vanessa enjoyed the moment, enjoyed watching the interaction, thinking that Tim was a pretty good father. He showed an awful lot of patience as Matthew threw questions his way and started to hurry and needed to be slowed down.

"The thing is, son, you're not going to be able to finish this tonight, so put the brakes on. The box says six hours. You don't have six hours before bedtime."

Matthew scowled but listened.

Vanessa finally volunteered a word of caution. "Six hours is actually optimistic, I think."

"I suspected." Tim smiled. "But if he doesn't want to mess this up, he can't rush no matter how long it takes. Right?"

Matthew nodded, echoing, "Right," as his brow furrowed and his tongue stuck out between his lips. His concentration was intense. From time to time he looked at the picture on the front of the box as if to assure himself that these pieces would eventually look like the photo.

Tim brought coffee for himself and Vanessa and milk for Matthew. He looked over his son's shoulder at the directions and remarked, "This is going to go together in pieces."

Matthew looked up. "What's that mean?"

"You've seen me build things. Well, this works the same. You're going to put the legs together. Then the feet. You'll connect them. Then the spine and tail. Then the head. When you get all those pieces done, it'll be time to put them all together."

"Okay," Matthew answered and returned to his work.

Vanessa spoke. "We have summer camps for kids. They come to the museum and work on projects. Anyway, some of them get seriously frustrated that they can't see it all go together at once."

"I won't," Matthew announced. "I know what Dad means."

Vanessa smiled at him, but he was too busy to notice. She glanced at Tim and caught him staring at her. The heat in his gaze was obvious, causing a pleasurable shiver to run through her. Almost at once he returned his attention to his son, but she hadn't missed the message. He wanted her.

The hard part was facing up to the fact that she wanted him, too.

Matthew had painstakingly organized all the pieces on the dining table before Tim sent him up to bed. He seemed resigned to being unable to put any of it together until tomorrow, but he wasn't difficult about it.

"This is going to be so cool," was the last thing he said to his father as Tim switched off the light and left the room.

"So cool indeed," Tim responded as he shut the door.

Downstairs he found Vanessa still sitting at the table, looking at all the carefully laid out pieces. "He's going to be like you," she remarked. "I've rarely seen that much organization from a boy his age."

"Well, you gave him a really great present. He thinks it so very cool, according to him. So thank you, Vannie."

She smiled at him. "My pleasure. I never fail to get a kick seeing a child excited by science…even if it's a wooden puzzle."

"I know he can barely stand waiting to see it finished. Half the fun is getting there, though. I hope he's beginning to learn that."

"A lot of us never learn that." She leaned back in her chair and stretched a bit. "I need to move."

"Pace if you feel like it. Or we can move to another room. These dining chairs weren't exactly designed to sit on for a long time."

He hoped he wasn't imagining that she was relaxing with him again. The past few days had been uncomfortable while she tried to keep her distance and he tried to give it to her. They were together almost all the time. How much better if they could just relax.

She opted for the living room. He was sure after the days they'd spent scraping, peeling and carting, she probably felt physically tired. He was used to it, but he doubted she was. Her lab job must be largely sedentary.

"Why did you decide to leave excavating the fossils?" he asked. "I know you said it was hard work, and the lab is more exciting, but I think I'd be happier with the physical activity."

"Digging was hot and dusty, like I said. Discovery was as exciting as anything could be. But I realized after a few years that I was thinking more about the questions attached to each bone than about the work in progress. I'm fortunate, though. Our museum supports a number of digs, so if I wanted to take a turn at it again, I could."

"I think I'd like to try my hand at it. I'm sure Matthew would, although he might get bored fast."

"Maybe so. Every dig I was on started with a spectacular find of some kind, some bone jutting out of recently washed-away earth or recently revealed limestone. Still, after the first few exciting weeks, things would usually slow to a crawl while we hunted around for other finds. Finding a complete skeleton is extremely rare, because after the animal died, its remains were subjected to the elements and carrion eaters. So bones got washed away, rolled around, worn away, and only some of them would end up in a situation good enough to preserve them, if any of them did. While it may seem like we find loads of fossils, the truth is they're rare. Compared to the numbers of animals that must have roamed this planet, the fossils are few and far between."

"I guess so. But if they weren't we'd be tripping over them all the time."

She laughed, the sound pleasing him.

"What got you into this field?"

"Partly that when I was kid we lived for a while in upstate New York. Our driveway was gravel and the gravel was full of seashells. That rock came from a nearby quarry, so I asked about the shells in school and was told that long ago the whole area had been under the sea. That stuck with me enough that I got truly curious. When the school took us to the Museum of Natural History in New York City, the bones won the day. It was all I could think about doing when I got to college."

He wondered what things might strike Matthew that way, or if he'd even know until much later. Of course, nothing might strike him that way at all. If there was one thing he'd learned from his son, it was that interests could pass rapidly and be forgotten in the changing of the days and his age. Watching his son grow was the biggest adventure in his life.

"Anyway," she continued, "I was lucky, too. I went to college on a full scholarship. I discovered an aptitude for geology, which really helps in this field, and pale-ontology seemed to be in my own bones."

"A full scholarship?" he repeated. "How many brains have you got tucked in that head?"

She blushed faintly. "Enough."

"Well, I guess so. I knew you were smart, but wow."

He could tell he was making her uneasy, so he dropped it, but that didn't mean he wasn't impressed. He'd gotten to college the hard way: on loans and money from working for his father.

"I wouldn't have been able to go any other way," she said after a moment. "I worked, but that had to help out at home. So I was very, very lucky."

"I didn't finish college," he admitted. "Three years in, my dad was injured on the job, and he needed me to take over. And frankly, given that I had a company to take over, school seemed increasingly irrelevant. Dad wanted me to finish, but I didn't want him spending his savings on hiring someone to do what I could do. I'm glad I didn't. He and Mom were able to follow their dream and travel. I doubt they'd have been able to do that if I'd stayed in college. The way it turned out, they had enough savings to go, and I was able to send them a bit every month to keep them going."

She looked at him, her expression a mixture he couldn't quite read. "You did a remarkable thing."

He shrugged it off. "We do what we need to do. That was the right decision. Easy as rolling off a log, so I've got no complaints."

Except for Claire, he thought with the inevitable twinge of loss and sorrow. Since her passing, he'd been short on dreams. Very short. All he wanted was to see Matthew grown and ready to stand on his own two feet. Then…well, then maybe he'd find he could dream again. But once upon a time, all his dreams had been wrapped around Claire. More children. A houseful of grandchildren eventually. Big family holidays. Eventually retiring to sit on the porch of a summer evening holding his wife's hand as night fell. Simple dreams, gone now.

He'd never wanted a great adventure, had never wanted to leave his mark on the world in some fashion. That probably made him boring, but it also had made him content.

Now he was sharing a sofa with an extremely bright woman who probably had bigger dreams.

"Vanessa? Do you have dreams?"

"Dreams?" She looked perplexed.

"About where you want to be down the road. Ambitions. Director of something? Make a discovery that changes everything in your field?"

"Those big things are few and far between. Progress

comes in small increments most of the time. If I can add an increment or two, I'll be happy."

That sounded reasonable enough. Why that relieved him he couldn't have said.

"What about you?" she asked.

"I want to see Matt grow up. Then I'll consider other things. I don't seem to be very ambitious."

"I think you're plenty ambitious. You want to raise your son. Isn't that big enough?"

"I think so. Others may not agree."

She shook her head a little. "I wish my dad had been concerned about seeing me grow up. His money and his reputation were more important. Maybe I learned something from that. Maybe all the wrong things, but I learned. Money's not that important. As for reputation... well, you spend your whole life building that, and one mistake doesn't have to ruin you forever."

He felt his brows rise. "That's a strong criticism of him."

"He deserves it," she said, a note of anger creeping into her voice. "He might as well have ditched my mother and me. At least then we wouldn't have had to watch him drink himself to death. Anyway, I can get that it hurt like hell to lose the family ranch, but that didn't make him a failure. Drinking made him a failure."

Once again he felt his heart squeeze with pain for her. This woman was still suffering in quite a few ways. He waited for her to let the demons escape in any way she decided.

But then she changed tack. "Anyway," she said, "I think you've chosen a great path. Matthew's an amazing boy, and he seems totally secure. I can't imagine how wonderful that must feel, but I'm very glad he doesn't have to question it."

"And here I was feeling boring and unadventurous."

She smiled, the last anger vanishing from her expression. "Raising a child is the most important thing anyone can do in life. Doing it right is the best thing. You appear to be doing it right. Pat your back, Tim."

"I'm a long way from being able to do that," he said lightly. "Check back with me when he's thirty. But even then it won't be all my doing. Kids are born with their own personalities, and I have no doubt he'll do most of the hard work himself. All I can do is guide a bit."

Her expression shifted, and she looked away. Had he just put his foot in it again? Probably. He had no idea just how much she blamed her father for. How many scars he had left her with. "You've turned out pretty good," he said cautiously. "I think *you* get all the credit."

At that she smiled crookedly. "There were others along the way. Teachers and so on."

"I'm glad you had them."

"So am I. Anyway, I don't want to go over that all again. I've spent most of this week wrestling with myself, and I'm tired of it. I am who I am. I'm not going to be able to rearrange myself in one fell swoop."

"Why do you want to do that? Because coming back here stirred up old memories?" He felt his heart quicken as he waited for her answer. Why it should matter so much to him, he couldn't imagine. Especially since she was right. If she wanted to change, it was going to take a long time.

"I don't even know if it's possible for me to change,"

she answered slowly. "It's just that I've been thinking that living Rapunzel's life may be safe, but maybe it's not as interesting."

"Rumpelstiltskin could always show up."

At last she laughed. "But will he turn into Prince Charming?"

His heart hit full gallop, and he wondered if he was losing his mind. "Do you want a Prince Charming?"

"No," she said, unwittingly making his heart plummet. Then she picked it up again. "If I ever get close enough to someone, I'd just like him to be nice, reliable and good to be around. I don't want perfection, and I don't want some guy who spends hours in front of a mirror working out."

It was his turn to laugh. "I can understand that. But was Prince Charming that bad?"

"Think about his name," she said drily. "It tells the whole story right there. I know it's a fairy tale, but who would name their baby Charming?"

"Or their daughter Beauty."

They both started to laugh. "Yeah," she said on a giggle. "They couldn't have named her *Sleeping* Beauty unless they plotted against her from birth." Then she caught her breath. "Oh, I probably just offended a bunch of people."

"I'm the only one who heard you. Maybe some girls are named Beauty. It actually wouldn't be bad unless the poor child turns out homely. But Charming?"

"Don't bet against it. Unusual names seem popular now. Matthew will probably never know how lucky he is that you gave him such an ordinary, familiar name."

"No, he'll just grow up and go to court to change it."

That sent her into more laughter. When they calmed again, they were both a bit breathless. And then their eyes met.

In an instant Tim found it hard to breathe. The laughter had done to her what nothing else seemed able to do. She looked utterly relaxed, soft, open. Unguarded.

He wanted so badly to reach out to her, to kiss her, to just hold her. He was sure she wouldn't allow more than that, but he was almost as certain she wouldn't accept his embrace. He reminded himself how she had reacted to his kiss. And certainly her mention of repeating it had been a moment of impulse on her part.

Or maybe she was actually changing, just a tiny bit. Maybe in the midst of giving herself all that distance, she had been working away at something. She'd said, after all, that she was thinking about change.

Easy, boy. True change would take time. It wouldn't happen before she went home. At most he was seeing a few cracks in her armor, but he was glad to see them.

Then she reached out and touched his forearm. Rockets exploded in his head as he looked down at her hand. What was she about? She'd never touched him freely by herself. In fact, she had always seemed to avoid it.

He raised his gaze to hers and read an almost painful hope there, along with desire. "Vannie?"

"I guess I'm crazy, but I want to know…"

Her heart beat as rapidly as a sewing machine. Was she really doing this? Reaching out to a man for his touches, his kisses? Who knew where that would lead? Somewhere bad, she'd always told herself, but Tim seemed to be changing her irresistibly. He pulled her, drew her, touched her in long untouched places. Seeing him with his son had proved to her that he was none of the things she had feared.

Trying to steady her breath, she didn't complete her sentence. More avoidance. Talk about everything except a growing hunger that might consume her. "My dad threw himself away because he lost a ranch. You lost your wife but kept yourself together."

"For my son," he reminded her.

She shook her head as an ache blossomed in her heart. "Don't you see, Tim? My dad had me. He had my mother. He had a whole lot more reason to carry on, but he didn't."

He didn't answer. Not that she really expected him to respond to a statement like that. What could he say? But her heart continued to hammer rapidly, and she felt as if she stood at a cliff edge, ready to take a leap.

God, this could be such a huge mistake. She looked at her hand, tried to make herself pull it back, but she couldn't. She wanted more than that simple touch but scarcely knew how to ask for it.

He probably wouldn't really want to give her any more, anyway. After the way she'd been acting for a week? After the way she'd fled after he kissed her? She wasn't blinded by her scars, and she could read in his occasional glance that he wanted her. Or at least he was attracted.

But handling her must strike him as about as safe as handling nitroglycerin. Even sitting here filled with yearning, she couldn't guarantee to herself or him that she wouldn't suddenly panic and run.

"I'm such a mess," she murmured.

"Oh, Vannie, just shut up," he said.

Startled, she barely had time to register his words before he pulled her over so she sat across his lap and silenced her by covering her mouth with his.

Some corner of her mind registered that he was man-handling her, but the biggest part of her didn't care. In fact, the biggest part of her was thrilled that he'd taken the leap for her.

She let her head fall back against his arm and opened her mouth, giving him entry to a place no one had been allowed before. The few times she'd kissed, except for the other day, the experience had left her wondering what all the hoopla was about.

She knew now. As his tongue explored the delicate inside of her mouth, warmth began to pour through her, filling her like hot honey until she felt soft, safe and eager.

If that kiss had lasted for an eternity, she wouldn't have objected. Her arm crept up until her hand wrapped around the back of his neck, holding him close. *Don't stop. Oh, please, don't stop.*

He didn't seem ready to. His lips lifted as his free hand crept up toward her breast and cupped it with a gentle squeeze. She caught her breath as pinwheels of light exploded behind her eyes and warmth began to transmute into sizzling heat. Was that her saying his name breathlessly over and over?

Then his mouth returned to hers, and this time his tongue plundered her, striking a rhythm that caused her whole body to clench in response. His hand began brushing over her breast, over her hardening nipple, and she shivered with pleasure.

Why had she avoided this her entire life? The question blew away on the storm of passion he was unleashing in her, a storm that was rapidly turning her into putty in his hands. Her hand slipped from his neck to his shoulder, her fingers digging in as if she were afraid she might fall.

A tornado of pleasure whipped inside her, sensations beyond imagining, and she wanted more. So much more. A throbbing heaviness between her thighs seemed to be seeking an answer of some kind. She felt so empty and full at the same time.

Then the doorbell rang.

Chapter Nine

"Aw, hell," Tim said, after ripping his mouth from hers. He froze. Maybe they'd go away. Looking down at Vannie's sleepy face and slightly swollen mouth, he wished the visitor to the devil.

The bell rang again. Damn it. Then from upstairs he heard Matthew's sleepy voice.

"You okay, Daddy?"

His voice cracked as he said, "Fine. Go back to bed, buddy."

He looked down at Vanessa again and saw awareness brightening her eyes. Then saw them widen.

"Oh!" she said and squirmed quickly off his lap.

That only made him ache harder. "Damn," he said aloud.

"Matthew," she whispered as she tried to straighten

a shirt he hadn't been able to rumple enough yet to need it.

"Yeah. Best birth control in the world. A kid."

Astonishing him, a small giggle escaped her. "And someone who keeps ringing the doorbell."

As if in answer to her statement, it rang again.

"God, I'm going to have some words for whoever it is. It's after ten o'clock."

"Maybe something's wrong."

That possibility was the only reason he forced himself to stand and walk over to answer it. He had the awful feeling that an opportunity had just been lost forever.

When he opened the door, he was not pleased to see Larry standing there. "What's the matter?" he demanded. "You didn't attack Vanessa enough last time? You need to draw more blood?"

"No," Larry said. "I shouldn't have... I just wanted her to know I'm sorry." He looked past Tim, and by the way his eyes widened, Tim knew he saw Vanessa.

She spoke, surprising him. "Forget it, Larry. I've said plenty of bad things about my father."

"I'm not going to forget it. I was wrong. Like you had any more to do with all that than I did."

The wind was blowing in through the door, chilling the house rapidly. Much as he didn't feel like it, Tim stepped back. "Get in here. My heating bill can't take this."

Larry crossed the threshold, taking two steps so that Tim could close the door behind him. Then he grudgingly offered the guy some hot coffee. Maybe it would be good for Vanessa if Larry really *had* had a change of heart.

"Thanks," Larry said. "It's colder than…" He broke off, stifling the bawdy line. Then he asked, "Is it really that cold anymore? Look at the Arctic."

Tim let himself relax a bit. "It's cold *here* tonight," was his answer. "Come into the kitchen, if that's okay with you, Vanessa."

"It's fine. Maybe Larry and I could use a little talk."

Larry followed them into the kitchen while unzipping his jacket but not removing it. "I'd've come sooner, but I just got back in town a half hour ago." He settled into one of the kitchen chairs while Tim started the pot of coffee he'd set up for morning brewing.

Vanessa sat across from Larry, glad that would put Tim in the middle, the place usually enjoyed by Matt. She was willing to give this a shot, but old, familiar tensions were already settling into her bones. Larry had proved her every fear right, and she could feel her walls slamming into place, preparing for another verbal assault.

For the first time she regretted those walls. Just a few minutes ago, they had been crumbling before the gentle onslaught of Tim's sexual advances, and she'd been feeling so good. Now she was faced with the nightmare of the past again.

Nobody spoke while the coffeepot steamed and water dripped into the carafe below. Studying Larry, Vanessa realized he was as uncomfortable as she was.

At last Tim poured coffee for all of them and took

the remaining chair. "Are we just going to sit here?" he asked.

Vanessa looked at him, sensing his impatience. Well, she felt impatient, too, considering what Larry had interrupted, but she felt a strong need to finish this, and here was her opportunity.

"I guess I should start," Larry said. "My dad was angry about what happened, about what Bob did. And he blamed your father for drawing him into it. So when I heard you were in town, I blew up. I'm sorry."

"I'm not any happier with my father," Vanessa said. Might as well admit it. The man's conduct had shadowed most of her life.

Larry grimaced. "I told my mother what I'd done when I called her from the road. If she'd been close, she might have skinned me."

"Why?" Vanessa asked as anxiety began to rise in her. Her least favorite subject, yet one she hadn't been able to get out of her mind since facing the fact that she had to come here. "Everyone probably thought the same things your father did."

Larry shook his head. "Not according to my mother. First she ragged on me for attacking you. You were just a kid, she said, no older than me. You didn't have a thing to do with what happened."

"Very true," Tim remarked. Vanessa saw him relaxing, leaning back in his chair as he sipped coffee.

"Exactly. When she said that, well, I didn't need her to say anything else. I felt truly stupid. And bad. Then she told me something I didn't know because I'd never talked to her about it." He paused, lifting his mug of coffee and nearly draining it in on long draft.

"What was that?" Vanessa prompted.

Larry put down his mug and looked her straight in the eye. "She said nobody talked my dad into giving all that money to Bob. Nobody but Bob. She tried to talk him out of it again and again, warning him it was dangerous to put all his eggs in one basket. He was hell-bent on making money. She told me all his talk about it being your father's fault as much as Bob's was just because he felt like an idiot, he was furious and he wanted to blame someone. Bob got arrested, but your father left town. Apparently my dad thought yours got off scot-free. But as my mother reminded me, your dad lost his whole ranch. Not exactly scot-free."

"Not exactly," Vanessa agreed. Tension had filled her as it always did when this subject came up. She wished she could just release it, like air from a balloon. She wanted this to be over, but Larry had been strong enough and kind enough to come apologize for his outburst, and surely she owed him something. But what? "My dad was pretty messed up, too," she said finally. "He lost every job he ever had and drank himself to death."

Larry nodded. "I'm sorry. That's pretty bad. Then I show up like an idiot and yell at you. My mother was right. You were just a kid. I was just a kid. It's not up to either of us to pay for what they did, right or wrong. It's not like we could have stopped it."

Vanessa drew a breath and decided to share her part of the truth with him. "My dad believed everyone here hated him."

Larry shook his head. "Then I drop on you like that? I guess there aren't enough apologies for me to make.

As far as I know, my dad was the only guy who blamed your dad. I never heard a word of that from anyone else."

He paused, drummed his fingers on the table briefly, then pushed back and stood. "I guess both of us had messed-up fathers. And my mother is right. We shouldn't let them mess us up anymore."

"Wise woman," Vanessa said, wishing she could feel relief in her heart.

"Yeah, she usually is. Sorry for breaking up your evening, but the need to apologize was riding me. Maybe I'll see you around sometime."

Then he headed for the door. Tim went to show him out while Vanessa remained at the table.

When Tim returned, he brought a draft of cold air with him. "That might not have been an emergency, but I'm glad he stopped by anyway. You needed to hear that."

"Maybe so," she said, and a long sigh escaped her. "I put it all behind me, Tim. I really did. Until Earl called and told me about the house. Then it came rushing back like a runaway train. All the old feelings, the fears, the anger. As fresh as it had ever been."

"Then Larry."

"Then Larry," she agreed. "But even so, even as I've been running the maze inside my head trying to change myself, the thing is..."

"What?" he prompted eventually.

"I think scraping the walls in that house has been more therapeutic."

"Really?"

She smiled faintly. "Yeah. Really. Every time I pull

wallpaper down, it feels good. Like ripping up the past. So who knows? Maybe I *am* finally getting past it all. It might not change my personality, but maybe I can get rid of leftover anger and hurt."

"I hope so. And by the way, there's nothing wrong with your personality."

"I wish I believed that."

"You will when the anger's gone. Anyway, just ask Matthew what he thinks about your personality. I happen to know he likes you."

"The feeling is mutual." But that wasn't the thing topmost in her mind. Topmost was that an exquisite moment had passed. Larry had driven away the heated mist of desire that had overtaken her, that had lifted her so far out of herself that she felt like someone else. Deep inside, she knew she couldn't call it back. Not now.

Even from the grave her father had done it again.

"I think I'll go to bed," she said, rising. The turmoil and anger were back, not as bad, but bad enough to get in the way of anything else. "See you in the morning, Tim."

Tim listened to her walk down the hall. He was straddling two contradictory emotional states, and neither one was doing him a bit of good. He wanted to follow her down that hall and climb into bed with her and show her how good life could be. The other part of him felt that would now be a terrible intrusion.

Apology notwithstanding, Larry had reopened the very things that had been holding her apart from the start. She had been about to close the door on them, at least for a little while, when he'd arrived to shove it open once more.

Hell. Selfish as it was, he was still aflame with hunger for that woman, and no matter how much he told himself it was pointless and she didn't really want it, he couldn't smother it.

Not since Claire had he come as alive has he had been growing since Vanessa arrived. Why couldn't he have reacted this way to a woman who didn't have major problems to deal with? Why this woman?

It wasn't just that she was beautiful in a restrained way. Or that she was essentially kind, to judge by her treatment of Matthew and her willingness to talk to a classroom full of kids. Was it because he felt the same hollowness inside her that had afflicted him since Claire had died?

Well, that would be a royally stupid reason to get together. Damn, he knew perfectly well that no person on the planet could be expected to fill the empty holes in another. Nobody could replace Claire, and he didn't want it. Her place in his heart would always remain.

The emptiness in Vanessa...if she didn't figure out how to fill it on her own, he couldn't do it for her. Life just didn't work that way.

You made room in your heart for someone—you didn't patch it with them.

Maybe Larry's interruption had been a good thing. Maybe it had saved him and Vanessa from making a mistake.

If so, then why didn't he feel like it?

Cussing mildly under his breath, he dumped all the coffee and prepared the pot once again for morning.

She'd be gone in little over a week. Things would return to normal.

But he was going to miss her anyway.

The next two days passed in a haze of hard work. Nothing sexual reared its head, but maybe that was because they both worked harder than ever. They got the walls ready to paint. They debated whether to pull out the floor tiles that looked so dingy or if they could be saved by a thorough cleaning. They talked about new bathroom and kitchen fixtures.

Tim kept thinking of what he'd do if he owned this house. Maybe he ought to buy it, but he didn't suggest it to Vanessa. Somehow he didn't want to attach himself to her nightmare memories.

Vanessa announced she was speaking at the school on Monday, just after lunch, laughing as she said, "I guess it'll be my job to keep the kids awake."

Judging by Matthew's response to her stories, Tim figured that wasn't going to be a problem.

He swiped his spackle knife over the last patch on an upstairs wall and stood back. "Tomorrow morning," he said.

"What?" she asked.

He wondered if she had any idea how cute she looked with a bandanna over her hair, wearing a spackle-stained plaid shirt and jeans that were beginning to look as if they belonged to a serious construction worker.

"Saturday," he said, even though she knew. "A good day to go to the paint store and pick the colors you want to slap on these walls."

She chewed her lower lip. "Shouldn't we go with

plain white? Not that I'd want that, but any colors I pick might turn off a potential buyer."

He used the butt of the spackle knife to hammer the can closed. "If you talk to a real estate agent, you'll discover that one of the things we're going to do is make this house look like someone lives here. If you care how much you get for it, anyway. After all this work, you should."

She hesitated, looking around. "It doesn't feel like Bob's house any longer. It's as if working on it has made it *my* house."

He smiled. "Then choose your own colors, woman."

She laughed. "Okay."

They went downstairs. All the overhead lights were on along with a few work lights, and she leaned against the counter as he washed the spackle knife.

"What else would you do to this place if it were your own?"

"The kitchen," she said promptly. "New countertops, new appliances. And I might paint the cabinets, or just remove most of the doors."

He looked around. "I've got some used cabinets in a storage room that you might like. Much better condition than these."

She opened one of the doors. "You think the whole thing needs to be replaced?"

He came over to stand by her and point. "Water damage at the back of them. It doesn't look bad, but if we get into the cabinets, I might not like what we find behind them. If it's just the cabinets themselves, I can fix it with a little sanding and refinishing."

Inadvertently he brushed against her and heard her

quickly indrawn breath. Heat surged in him, and he backed away.

She remained staring into the cabinet, frozen. After a few second she spoke. "I wouldn't want to leave a mess for the new owner."

"If I pull one of these down, we're going to have to do it all. So come with me to storage tomorrow and see if you like the cabinets I have."

"Okay." She closed the door. "My list seems to be growing."

"Mainly because you've got a lot of sweat equity in this place. You'll get over it."

At that she laughed and helped him clean up, readying for the next workday there.

That afternoon, Matt came home from school announcing that he'd been invited to spend Saturday night with Jimmy Jackson. "Can I go? Can I take my dinosaur puzzle, too? He wants to see it."

Tim hesitated. "I'd hate for it to get broken."

"I can take the one I haven't started yet. We can sort the pieces."

Tim glanced at Vanessa. She'd gone to a lot of trouble to get his son those puzzles.

"I can always replace it," she said. "Don't worry about that."

Tim squatted until he was on eye level with Matthew. "Okay then. But be very careful and don't lose pieces. It was nice of Vannie to get them for you, and I'd really hate to ask her to do it again."

"I'll be careful," Matthew said stoutly. "So will Jimmy. He already promised."

"Okay then. When are you supposed to go over there?"

Matthew furrowed his brow. "Jimmy said you need to check with his mom."

"Ah. So the two of you outlaws plotted this today?"

Matthew grinned sheepishly. "Sort of."

Tim straightened. "I guess I need to check with Mrs. Jackson, then."

"Does this happen often?" Vanessa asked as Matthew trudged with his backpack into the dining room.

"Not that often, but much better than when he was five and brought Jimmy home from school with him and nobody had bothered to tell Jimmy's mom where he'd gone. We all learned from that escapade."

"I bet."

"Life with kids," Tim said easily. "You learn a lot. Listen, if you want to go shower, I'll just check on that roast I've been marinating."

That morning he'd put a pork roast in some balsamic vinaigrette, sealed it in a plastic bag and had let it soak all day. Usually he was left with enough after cooking the portion of tenderloin to make sandwiches for a day or two, but he suspected there'd be no leftovers this time. Everyone liked his roast made this way.

He glanced at the clock and decided he had an hour before he needed to pop it in the oven. Plenty of time to call Jimmy's mom and see what she thought of this overnighter. Or if she'd even heard of it yet. Then he'd hit the shower himself and get ready for a pleasant evening.

He always enjoyed evenings with his son and figured there'd be far fewer of them as time passed. Enjoy it while you had it was his motto. He picked up the phone. Not surprisingly, the Jacksons' number was on auto-dial. Jimmy and Matthew had been as thick as thieves forever.

"Hi, Mims," he said when she answered. "Tim Dawson. I wonder if you've heard the latest plans the boys have made."

She laughed. "I was just being informed. Sleepover here tomorrow night?"

"That's what I was told."

"It's fine with me. Bring Matthew over around two if you can. I'd like the two of them to wear themselves out so they're not up all night."

He chuckled. "Good plan. I hope it works."

"They're still young enough that no matter how hard they try not to, along about ten or so, as long as I have them in sleeping bags, they'll sleep in front of some movie. And I always pick a movie they know well so it won't keep them awake."

"I need to remember that. Okay then. I get the next round."

"Don't you always?"

He was smiling as he hung up. He liked Mims Jackson a whole lot and had ever since junior high when, for the first time, he'd noticed she was a girl. He'd been a lovesick puppy for all of three weeks, but then someone else had caught her eye, and he, oddly enough, had felt almost relieved to get back to his guy friends. He'd felt cut off during that brief, intense relationship.

It had been another three years before a girl had crossed his radar in a way that made him want to try again. That girl had been Claire.

He was looking through his freezer at vegetables, trying to decide which ones he wanted tonight, when he heard a sound and turned. Vanessa had made quick work of her shower. She was wearing a fresh green sweatshirt and fleece pants, her feet covered by black ballet slippers. A towel still wrapped her head.

"That felt *good*." She smiled. "Is the weather taking a turn? Back in the bedroom the wind sounded strong."

"I don't know," he admitted. "I suppose I should check. If Matthew's going to miss his sleepover, I don't want the news to hit him at the last minute. So do you have any preference for veggies tonight? I think I have just about every kind frozen."

"What does Matthew like?"

He looked at her over his shoulder and remarked drily, "I believe I asked for your preferences. He likes just about everything."

"Broccoli?" she asked, hoping Matthew didn't hate it.

"That's probably what he would have asked for. Okay, I've got plenty. Feel like peeling some potatoes? Matthew loved them mashed."

"Glad to help."

He set her up, then announced he was going to shower. The need to escape had been growing stronger since the scents of soap and shampoo had begun reaching him. From there it was a small step to imagining her skin, soft and still slightly moist from the shower. Then another small leap and he'd be in trouble.

The demons of desire were flogging him again, and he couldn't let them take charge. Since the other night when they'd come perilously close to going all the way, he'd felt like he'd gone too far. She was happy and relaxed when they were working, and ever so slightly nervous in the evening when Matt went to bed. Dang, did she think he was going to just pounce on her?

Well, maybe she had a right to worry, he thought as he climbed the stairs to go clean up. After all, he'd told her to shut up then dragged her into his lap like some kind of caveman. Finesse. He needed to find some finesse. He also needed to remember that this woman needed space, and he needed to stay clear as much for her sake as anything.

He should keep his attention on the job. It had been kind of fun, though, to watch her gradual change in attitude toward the house as she helped strip it down to bare walls. She seemed to have taken it away from Bob, at least emotionally, and made it somewhat her own.

Like that discussion of kitchen cabinets, and the changes she'd want to the kitchen if it was her place. When she'd arrived in town, she probably would have been unable to consider the house in that light, even to pretend. Now she was seeing the kitchen as it could be.

Larry, too, in the end had wound up being good for her. His apology and recognition that they'd both been too young to be responsible for anything their fathers had done had probably reinforced her slow healing from the past.

It still appalled him, though, that any father could have forgotten his responsibilities like that. Vanessa's father had been a weak man in the ways that counted.

But when Tim looked a Vanessa, he saw a remarkably strong woman. She might claim that her upbringing had turned her into an introvert, and maybe it had.

Certainly she seemed more comfortable with an emotional distance.

But a few times she'd let those barriers fall—mostly with Matthew, occasionally with him. Maybe the fear of loss and judgment that had been instilled in her for so many years was loosening its grasp.

He hoped so. She deserved a life full of people who cared about her and about whom she cared.

But his meanderings were pointless. He had a job to do for her, and they'd probably both be better off if he just paid attention to it. Rapunzel was entitled to her tower for as long as she felt she needed it, and he was no Rumpelstiltskin to steal his way in and demand something from her.

Thank goodness for the dinosaur puzzles. They'd been making the evenings much more relaxed than they might have been otherwise. Especially since he'd crossed the line the other night.

Oh, yeah, especially since then.

Matthew, ever the bundle of energy, was eager to join Tim and Vanessa in the morning on a trip to the storage room to look at the cabinets and to the paint store to look for swatches. The whole thing sounded like a great deal of fun to him.

Vanessa was glad he wanted to go. He made her feel comfortable, and with his chatter eased her past moments where she started to feel awkward for no reason than her own hang-ups.

The storage facility was behind a garage and car rental place not far from the train tracks. The building wasn't huge, but it was big enough that Tim had been able to rent a climate-controlled garage-size unit to stash the cabinets and other things he didn't want exposed to temperature and humidity changes.

She definitely liked the cabinets, as he'd promised. Much nicer than the ones already in place, and they looked new.

"Where did you get these?" she asked.

"Somebody ordered them and then didn't want them after all. So I picked them up for a song. I can modify them to fit easily enough."

"I like them," she said with certainty as she ran her hands over them. The wood might or might not have been the currently favored color, but she liked the warm mahogany look of them. "I love them," she said a minute later. "Just love them."

"Then I'll put them in. I just wish you'd be the one enjoying them." Vanessa, who had just started to wonder what he meant by that, was glad when he turned swiftly to point at some furniture. "Some near antiques we can put in the house if you want to make it look occupied. A loaner. My in-laws left the stuff behind when they jumped ship."

Matthew, who'd been looking into spaces behind things, announced, "They didn't jump ship. They went to New Zealand. They live with hobbits."

Tim arched a brow. "Is that what they told you?"

"They sent me a picture of a hobbit house under a hill."

Vanessa had to cover her mouth with her hand. Tim looked thunderstruck. "So…what exactly did they tell you?"

Matthew shrugged. "It was a postcard in a letter

they sent. They didn't say much, but the postcard said it was the Underhill hobbit house. So I looked up hobbits. They aren't much bigger than me."

"Oh, boy," Tim said under his breath, then asked, "You looked up hobbits?"

"Sure. They look funny, though, with all that hair on their feet."

"I see. Son, we're going to have to talk about this later, but right now I need to get Vannie over to look at paint."

"Sure."

Apparently, a photo was too real to just deny, Vanessa thought, amused, as they piled into Tim's truck to head to the other end of town and the lumberyard and home improvement store. The place was huge but was locally owned, to judge by the sign. Hadn't Tim said he'd read the books to his son? In was interesting to her to watch the way Matthew could weave fiction and reality so seamlessly. Sure, the books were just a story, but now he had a photo of a hobbit house, and he'd looked up hobbits to learn about them. She figured it might be hard to walk that one back.

"Maybe I'd better avoid Harry Potter," Tim muttered as they drove toward the store.

"No, I wanna read it," Matthew said.

"Just so long as you understand it's all *pretend*."

"Of course," Matthew said. "Magic isn't real. But dinosaurs are!"

"Were," said Tim.

"They're not all dead," Matthew announced. "I talked to my teacher about it. Crocodiles. Alligators. And some kind of fish I can't remember."

"I guess I'm going to have to go back to school," Tim said as he turned into the parking lot.

But Matthew was looking at Vannie. "What's that fish?"

"Coelacanth," she answered promptly. "For a long time we thought they were extinct, but then some fishermen found one. Then later we found out they were commonly being eaten as food in some fishing villages near India and Indonesia."

Matthew giggled. "Then maybe a T. rex will show up someday."

Vanessa shuddered playfully. "I certainly hope not."

"Remind me not to let this boy watch *Jurassic Park*," Tim said as he stopped the truck and turned it off. "Next thing you know he'll be doing his own cloning."

The home improvement section of the sprawling store fascinated Vanessa. She'd never visited one before because she'd always lived in apartments that came with maintenance. She realized as she walked around that she could spend hours here taking it all in.

But Tim guided her over to the banks of paint chips, and she was off on a new dream. So many pretty colors in varying hues and shades. How was she going to make up her mind?

"You don't have to decide right now," Tim said. "We can take home as many chip samples as you want."

Well, that was an invitation to plunder, Vanessa thought. By the time she had every chip that interested her even mildly, she had quite a stack in her hand.

Tim was smiling. "Any others?"

"I think I just overwhelmed myself."

Then Matthew approached with a strip of dark blue

paints that didn't get very light and passed it to his father. "I want these colors in my bedroom."

Tim surveyed them. "Really? It'll be awfully dark."

"I know, like night. Then we can put glow-in-the-dark stars on the ceiling."

"Oh." Tim was clearly trying to hide a grin. "We'll think about that," he said, his tone sober.

Matthew looked at Vanessa. "When he says we'll think about it, that means he doesn't really like it."

Vanessa laughed. "You never know."

"True," said Tim. "I didn't say no."

Matthew brought his strip of paint chips along as they left and headed for home.

The trees were tossing more edgily, and the sky had turned a dark gray.

"Autumn," Tim remarked. "Very changeable. I read once that the worst time to sail is in late autumn or early spring, because the weather is so variable and could get bad without much warning. That could be true, I guess. All I know is our weather seems to be bouncing around this week."

When they pulled up at the house, Vanessa eyed the snowman they'd built. While it had done a good job of lasting, right now it was little more than a heap of snow surrounded by yellowed grass.

Inside, they went to the kitchen, where Tim set about making peanut butter sandwiches for whoever wanted them. Vanessa wasn't feeling at all hungry yet, but Matthew was. He acted as if eating would bring him to two o'clock faster.

He pushed his color chips her way. "Can you keep that for me?" he asked.

"I certainly will, but I doubt anything would happen to it anyway."

"Oh, I don't know," Tim remarked jokingly. "We do have the invisible man running around who loses my car keys and makes small toys disappear."

Matthew giggled. "Yeah. Only you forgot where you put your keys."

"Probably so."

Matthew gave Vanessa a knowing look. "I'm too old for that now."

"I can see that."

The boy was so charming she had the worst urge to hug him until he squeaked. She guessed he wouldn't like that at all, however. He seemed to be sprouting a good deal of independence from what she had seen.

After Matthew had his sandwich, Tim turned on the radio to listen to the weather report. High winds all day and through the night, occasional gusts up to fifty. A front was passing to the north, and they might see a little snow but not much.

"That's not too bad," Tim said. The report continued for another few seconds, warning of dropping temperatures on Sunday night. "Winter's moving in, I guess."

"Halloween in two weeks," Matthew said. "I hope it's not too cold for trick-or-treating."

"Too early to know," said his father. "But you know we'll set it all up in the gym if it's too cold to be out. You won't miss a single cavity."

Matthew's spirits, which were already high, rose even higher. He practically bounced up the stairs with his father to pack for his overnighter. Fifteen minutes later, they returned downstairs, Matthew with a packed backpack and Tim with a sleeping bag. Matthew had not forgotten the dinosaur puzzle and hurried into the dining room to get it.

"Want to ride along?" Tim asked as he opened the door to let Matthew through. "Five minutes. Hardly worth pulling on your jacket again unless there's something you want."

"I'll stay here."

She watched them leave, but as they did she felt loneliness step into her heart. Dang, what was going on inside her? She'd decided to quit worrying about the sense that something was wrong with her, that she wasn't standoffish by choice. Once she'd made up her mind to just *shut up*, as Tim had told her the other night, she'd let go of a whole bunch of tension.

But now she was feeling *lonely*? That wasn't like her. She usually loved her alone time and filled it with activities she enjoyed, whether reading a book, cooking a sinful dessert to take in for the office or planning her next vacation. She *liked* being by herself. Quiet time, time to just flow without pressure.

Now loneliness was an almost alien feeling to her as an adult. Settling at last at the kitchen table because the light was marginally better in here, even with the grayness of the day, she spread out the paint chips she had brought back with her and tried to imagine what colors she would paint the house.

She'd never had to make such a decision before. Every place she had ever lived had white walls in one state or another. The idea of splashing color all over a room excited her, especially since seeing the bedroom she was sleeping in here. Clearly Tim and Claire hadn't been afraid of color, and the lavender walls in there truly appealed to her.

It had to be Claire's doing, she thought. The room seemed to boast a feminine touch, although what did she know about that? She supposed guys could like lavender and forget-me-nots. Why not?

But then, with all the colors spread before her, she felt the loneliness again and wondered if this was a hint of what Tim felt with his wife gone. Maybe so. He certainly hadn't erased Claire from the house. He'd simply moved upstairs.

She glanced at the clock on the microwave and saw that it was well past the five minutes Tim had promised. Of course it was. He was a friendly man, and it would never occur to him to drop his son off at the door and drive away without at least some conversation.

All the colors of the rainbow lay before her, the entire spectrum, some bold and some soft and pale, but they were all there. She realized impulse had caused her to select the brightest colors, because when she tried to imagine painting a room in such a powerful shade, she had the feeling all it would do would be to shrink the room.

Paler colors, she decided, pushing away the strongest. But then she saw Matthew's selection again, the deep-as-night blues he had brought home. Down at the bottom of the strip the colors were suggested as trim paint for rooms painted in other shades.

She could imagine Tim being reluctant to turn his son's room into a cave, but the idea of glow-in-the-dark stars was exactly the thing to tickle a boy Matthew's age. Maybe he'd do it if it wouldn't be too hard to paint over at a later date. Or maybe Matthew would forget about it by next week. Sad to admit she had almost no knowledge of seven-year-olds. She really liked Matthew, though. The house felt empty without him, and the evening was probably going to be emptier without his cheery voice, his fascination with his dinosaur puzzles and his running commentary on just about everything.

Then she giggled, remembering the expression on Tim's face when his son had announced that he had a picture of a hobbit house and had looked up hobbits. There would be some untangling of fact and fiction in the future.

She was still smiling at the memory when Tim returned and walked in the door. He smiled immediately upon seeing her. Sloughing his jacket, hanging it and his keys on pegs beside the door, he waved at all the paint chips. "Did you make a decision?"

"Seriously? Only that I decided against the really intense colors. I think they'd be overpowering. Beyond that I don't know yet."

"It takes a while. If you narrow it down by Monday, I can pick up some sample cans and we can paint small patches of wall so you can see them in the rooms."

"You can do that?" So much she didn't know.

"Sure." He smiled, poured some of the coffee that was left and joined her at the table.

"It seems a lot to do when I'll be going home late next week." Her heart stuttered as she said it. Then she admitted, "I'm going to miss Matthew so much."

"He's going to miss you, too. No question. But, if you want, you can always fly back here to visit. The door's always open."

"Thanks." But he hadn't said he was going to miss her.

"You also don't have to pick any colors at all."

She looked at him. "But you said..."

"I know what I said. But I didn't mean for you to struggle with it. I just thought some colors might appeal to you for some of the rooms." He gave a light laugh. "Instead you came home with nearly everything."

She had to smile at that, sore as her heart felt right then. "Unlike Matthew, who's full of certainty. I never had to think about painting a room before. I'm an apartment dweller."

"Ah." He shook his head a little. "You've missed one of life's great pleasures, transforming a room with a coat of paint. Or maybe you've missed one of life's greatest disappointments. The color your bedroom is now? It didn't start that way. Claire changed it four times before she was finally happy with her color scheme."

"That must have been annoying."

"Not really. But that's why I like the idea of splashing samples on a wall. Until you see a color with natural lighting in the room you want to paint, it's hard to be sure."

She could understand that. "So about what Matt wants..."

"I may just do it, if he doesn't change his mind in the next few weeks."

"Really? You'd do that for him?"

His gaze settled on her, warm and amused. "I'd do a lot more for him, or for anyone I care about. This is just paint and stickers. When he tires of it, I can cover it all up easily enough. Paint isn't permanent."

The way he said it made her grin, too. "We certainly peeled enough of it away."

"Exactly. But his room wouldn't need that. A good coat of primer and I can change it to the next color he wants. The only thing I ever worry about with him is that he can be so changeable. I'd hate to paint that room next weekend only to have him decide while I was in the middle of it that he really wants gray walls."

A laugh escaped her, easing the strange feelings that had been swamping her. Loneliness? Really? Missing Matt…okay, that was at least understandable. The boy was a charmer, like his father.

But feeling saddened because Tim hadn't said he'd miss her, too? She had no right to that. None at all. He'd been wonderful to her, and she'd done everything except totally freeze him out.

Except for the other night. Warm memories of their embrace, his kisses, his touching her intimately, so sadly interrupted by Larry's arrival.

She realized she wanted to pick that up where they had left off. She wanted the experience even though nothing would ever come of it. Just remembering it made her insides squeeze pleasurably.

"I'm going to buy your house," he said unexpectedly. "I told you I thought it was time to move on, remember? Well, that house has great bones, and it's a bit bigger. Enough bigger that my office wouldn't have to be the size of a janitor's closet."

She gave a small laugh. "You do have a point there."

"A couple extra bedrooms would come in handy."

Given that there was one here that was more of a shrine, maybe so. He could have turned that into his office, but he hadn't. She was kind of surprised that he'd even let her use it. Maybe he *was* moving on.

"So, okay, let me help you with the colors. Since I'm going to buy it anyway."

Impulsively, as he reached for the color chips, she laid her hand over his. "Are you sure you want to do that? This isn't just to take a load off me, is it?"

He met her gaze. "I'm sure," he said quietly. "It's time. So let's look at these colors together."

Chapter Ten

Later the weather became nearly savage. The wind gusted so strongly that the windows rattled from time to time. Tim turned on more lights and listened every now and then to the sounds, cocking his head as if locating them.

"There's going to be a lot of work around here this week," he remarked. "Roofing. Probably some trees blown down. Not good."

"Are you worried about it?"

"Only for my neighbors. This place is sound enough. Your house...well, it's been a long time since the roof was replaced. We may have to do some reshingling."

"Why do I think that may cost more than I can afford?"

He shook his head. "Earl said the house was insured

when I asked him about weather damage I might find. If this wind messes up your roof, you'll be covered. Don't worry about it unless you need to for some reason."

She was willing to do that. One way or another, it wasn't going to be her headache for long. But Tim buying it? She thought he'd been joking the first time he'd suggested it. Ready to move on? What did that mean?

She suspected she'd just have to keep wondering.

By evening, the wind had quieted somewhat. It was still blowing, but without the big gusts. Tim made them a dinner of red beans and rice. The warm dinner was perfect, because even though the temperature in the house was fine, the sound of the wind made her feel chilled. Or maybe there were some drafts.

Tim chatted easily about random things, but he didn't seem uncomfortable when silence fell. She wished she could be so comfortable, but even after all this time with him, silences still made her feel awkward.

She might not be good at conversing and making deep connections with people, but she loved to listen to them talk. And for some weird reason, she felt that she was failing to step up when a conversation quieted and she didn't have anything to say. Except with her colleagues. Odd.

She liked to drift on other people's conversations. How very entertaining she must be.

She looked at the dozen or so strips of color chips they'd separated out between the two of them as being the most pleasing. The question now, she supposed, was which colors wouldn't jar if they could be seen in juxtaposition.

"Oh, my," she said suddenly, a memory striking her.

"What?" he asked.

"I just remembered. When I was in college, a friend's family painted their house. She dragged me over there to see it."

"You had a friend," he interrupted quietly.

"Well…we weren't terribly close. I told you I have trouble getting really close. But I can fake."

His brows lifted. "Okay. So the house?"

"She thought her mother had gone nuts. I wound up wondering if the woman was color-blind. We walked in the front door into the living room and everything, *everything*, straight back through the dining room, was a deep crimson. Powerful. But that wasn't where it got curious. My friend led me to the back of the living room where we could see the hall. It was awful. The hall was also crimson, but one of the bedrooms off it was painted bright orange, and the next one was apple green. It was a shocker."

"Sounds like it." A smile hovered around his lips. "Maybe nobody had ever let her have her way with color before."

"Or something. We hurried out and my friend just doubled over, laughing so hard. I had to laugh, too. She swore I was the only person she'd ever invite to see it."

"And you had a friend."

She nearly glared at him. "What are you pushing at, Tim?"

"That you had a friend. You keep saying you don't get close, but you had a friend. How close does someone have to be? Living in your pocket? In your thoughts constantly?"

"No. But when I left college, I didn't even miss her. That says something. I leave people behind all the time and I don't miss them. There's a part of me that never gets touched. That's all I was saying."

He nodded but looked as if he were weighing her words. "You said you'd miss Matthew."

Her heart jumped nervously, wondering where he was going. "I believe I will. I miss him already. I guess he's the exception. Tim, I told you I'm a wanderer. I pack up and move without looking back. If I ever had strong feelings for anyone—and I don't remember them if I did—they were gone as soon as I moved on."

"Uprooted too many times. Maybe the lack of grief when you moved on was the real protection, and not what came before."

She nearly sighed. "Does it make a difference?"

"A helluva difference," he said. "And who's deciding to do the moving since you got your job at the museum? You? So at this point you wouldn't even know how many friends you've made there that you *would* miss if you left." He shook his head a little.

"I've been thinking about this ever since I came back here, and I'm not getting anywhere with it," she told him. "I'm tired of trying to figure it out, and I doubt I'm going to change. It was only coming back here that made me wonder about it in the first place. Seeing Ashley. Seeing Bob's house and dealing with all that again. Realizing how hurt I'd been by everything that followed his deception and wondering how it had affected me. You'd be surprised how easy it is to go through the motions of what is expected and never really feel anything."

He tilted his head, his lips tightening a bit, and closed his eyes. She waited, but he didn't speak for a long time. And she was through talking about this. It wasn't helping, and she couldn't make it clear that she lacked something inside.

"I believe," he said eventually, his eyes opening slowly, "that life taught you to be very careful about how you spend your emotions. People are just going to be ripped from you sooner or later. Basic truism of life. But you had way too much of that as a child, so you're extra cautious. Giving little away that it would hurt to lose. But what makes you think you aren't like millions of other people? Most of us don't commit really deep feelings in the majority of our relationships. Nobody has the time or energy for that. Anyway, all I'm saying is give yourself a break. You don't need to change yourself if you don't want to. Happens I like you just fine already."

Sweet words, and they warmed her heart. But she still needed to be clear. "I'm saying, Tim, that when my parents died, I felt nothing. When my dog died, I cried. That's weird. And if I walked away from my job tomorrow, I'd miss the job, but after a few days wouldn't even think much about the people I'd left behind. That's weird, too."

He nodded. "Okay. But why is it so important to you all of sudden?"

"Because I don't think it's normal."

"Ah. I gathered that. But it's the way you are, for whatever reason, so just accept yourself. You're doing well, you're making the life you want. Nobody says you have to get close to anyone. If you're okay, why make a big deal of it?"

She looked down, realizing she was clenching her fingers so hard that they hurt. The problem was, she'd been okay until she got here. Until she'd walked into the bedroom he'd shared with his wife and had suddenly imagined what it might be like to have a truly intimate understanding with someone. To have a relationship worth grieving. Then, steadily, he'd been awakening desires in her for a closeness she'd always feared. And Matthew... God, to think she could miss having a child like him because of her walls. Somehow she didn't think she could fake a marriage the way she faked her friendships.

But he was saying something about that. About how not every relationship could be emotionally close. So maybe she wasn't faking all of it? Just because she didn't pour out her heart, or open it to everyone...

God, just let it go. The circle of her thoughts was closing around her like a noose, and she was really tired of it. He said she was fine. Apparently, she was going to continue being that way.

But there was another home truth, and hard though it was to speak it, she forced herself to do so.

"I would like, someday, to have a relationship like you have with your son. Like you probably had with your wife. And I'm not sure I'm capable of it."

"Now we're getting somewhere," he said gruffly.

Before she knew what he intended, he was scooping her off the chair and carrying her. Not upstairs, but back to the room he had shared with his wife. At least she thought he had.

He flipped on the light with his elbow and carried her to the bed, where he put her on the coverlet. Then he stood, hands on his narrow hips, looking down at her.

"This is the bedroom I shared with Claire. For a long time, I didn't want to change it, because when I walked in here I could almost feel her presence. Then I just closed the door on it, because it was as if I were holding both of us back."

"You and Matt?" she asked, her voice thick.

"Me and Claire. She's gone. She has a right to move on to her reward, not be held back by my grief. So, if I were holding her back, that wasn't good. Then I started thinking about Matthew and me, and how we needed to move on. There's just so long you can live in a mausoleum, Vanessa. This has been a lively one because of Matthew, but it's still a mausoleum."

She managed to swallow and absorb what he was saying. Moving on.

"Everyone has to move on sooner or later," he said. "Life doesn't let us hold still for long. I've been holding still in some ways. You've been moving on far too much. And worrying about it too much. So how about you and I see if we can meet somewhere in the middle?"

She cleared her throat. "I'm leaving..."

"I know you're leaving. And if you decide you never want to come back, I'll deal. Being geographically separated doesn't mean we can't connect emotionally. And I think the truth is, you're already connected to my son, and to me. Wanna deny it?"

She couldn't deny it. There was a lump growing in her throat, a very unusual sensation for her, as if tears wanted to roll. She almost never cried. Why did she feel like crying now?

She sat up, swinging her legs over the side of the bed, but she didn't leave. She looked up at him, wondering what was going on, because inside her she felt as if the earth were shaking and volcanoes were erupting. Strong feelings—the very kind of feelings she claimed not to have—were battering to be let out. All because of this man.

But what good would it do? "I don't understand you," she said.

"I'm saying that it's entirely possible to be close with someone who lives half a continent away. Distance can be either physical or emotional. It doesn't have to be both."

God, he looked almost iconic standing there with his hands on his hips, but then he moved, dropping to his knees in front of her. "Matthew likes you. He won't stop liking you because you go back to your job. If you send him a postcard from time to time, he won't forget you, either. I know my son."

The idea of sending postcards to Matthew didn't seem threatening at all. "I'd like to do that."

"So you can have a relationship with him. You could have one with me, too. Telephones, Skype and email all exist."

Despite the tightness in her throat, she felt like laughing, just a small bit. "And what kind of relationship would that be?"

"We'll just have to see. Right now I want to knock a few walls down by making love to you."

Her breath locked in her throat. Oh, man, she wanted that, too. Much as she'd been trying not to think about it, when he said it out loud, the desire to follow through overwhelmed her. Heat flowed through her veins, every nerve ending beginning to tingle in anticipation. Not even the memory of her one attempt at this, all the way back in college, could prevent the need from rising. Back then it had been awkward, inexperienced and ultimately unsatisfying, making her decide once was enough.

But it was different with Tim, for some reason. The longings she'd forced herself to bury until they hardly ever surfaced swept over her now, an irresistible tsunami of hunger.

Awash in powerful feelings, all her fears and objections were swept away. All she cared about was what this man was offering her right that moment. For once she didn't consciously or unconsciously count future costs. Past and future vanished in the incredible *now*.

She began to strip, wanting to get past this to what lay just ahead. She tugged her sweatshirt over her head and shimmied out of her fleece pants. When she straightened and cast aside her undergarments, she found flame burning in Tim's eyes.

"You're so beautiful," he murmured. But he didn't reach out to touch her. Instead, he pulled away his own clothes with impatience, tossing them without regard to where they fell.

Then they were locked in a primal space, both nude, anticipation so thick breathing became difficult. Vanessa's mouth went totally dry.

But it was a moment never to be repeated, and she knew it. She had free rein to look at him, to take in his broad shoulders, his narrow waist and flat belly, then…then…

She gasped with pleasure when she saw how ready he was for her. Reaching out like a child for candy, she closed her hand around his rigid member, feeling silky skin, a powerful pulse that caused him to move in her grip.

Tim closed his eyes, drawing several deep breaths, then opened them as he began to trace her with his fingertips.

The air almost seemed to pound with Vanessa's passion. Everything inside her quivered with longing and delight. His every light touch added flame to the heaviness of need that was overtaking her.

Her breasts became instruments on which he played a siren's song. His fingers slipped down to her middle, causing her to quiver.

She ran her free hand over him, too, testing muscle, feeling the nubs of his hardened nipples, reaching his hip and pulling because she wanted him even closer.

Then he slipped his hand between her legs and she crumpled, weakened by her hunger, weakened by his touch.

Tim felt her sag a little and caught her quickly, placing her supine on the bed. Her eyelids were heavy; her arms reached up for him.

He needed no further encouragement. He wanted this badly. Swinging himself onto the bed until he straddled her, he sought to learn her with his mouth, trailing his lips and tongue all over her.

She shivered as he licked her neck, but she bucked when he found the hardened berries of her nipples. His own passion throbbed so strongly that he didn't know how long he'd last. Nor was he worried about it. There were always second times in a night.

But the important thing was to make her feel everything he was feeling, to carry her into this powerful, almost painful but totally blissful experience with him.

As her body writhed beneath his touches, he knew she was with him, and his brain exploded with white-hot delight.

Thought was slipping away. Caution was slipping away. He searched out her every hill and hollow, and when his mouth found the cleft between her legs, she keened like a siren calling to him. Her nails digging into his shoulders told him all he needed to know.

One last moment of sense gripped him before it was too late. He leaned up and pulled open the drawer in a bedside table to get a condom.

Her eyes fluttered, and she saw it. Yanking it from his hand, she opened the package and pulled it out.

"Like this?" she whispered as she started to roll it on him.

"Yes..." Oh, man, it was too much, her delicate hands stroking him as she rolled it on, claiming him as much as he wanted to claim her.

"So sexy," she murmured, her voice cracking.

He tried to hold off a little longer, but he couldn't. He was locked in the grip of a hunger that now powered his world. Reaching down, he guided himself into her, feeling her warmth close snugly around him. He drew a sharp breath of pleasure, heard her mewl.

Then he reached up to hold her wrists and bent his head to kiss her breasts, sucking on them in rhythm to his movements.

Life took over, commanding, demanding. He couldn't have stopped for anything. This woman, this moment—nothing else mattered.

Vanessa saw pinwheels of color behind her eyelids, but she was hardly aware of them. She became ephemeral except for the feelings that tore her from earth and flung her to some other space with this man.

The heaviness between her legs, his weight there, seemed to fill an emptiness she hadn't been aware of until then. Everything left of thought, every part of her body, centered on the space between her legs, where a man now gave her the greatest gift and lifted her higher with every movement of his body.

Floating, struggling to a place she hardly knew, captive to the pain-pleasure that filled her. A pleasure so strong it almost hurt. More…more…

Then she reached the pinnacle and tumbled over into a gentler pleasure. But he didn't let her rest. He kept driving into her, and she began the climb again, hopeful, fearful she couldn't make it, then…

The entire universe exploded in a shower of stars. An instant later she heard Tim groan and shudder then collapse on her.

She lay limp, unable to even think. She had become experience, not thought, ruled by something beyond the mind.

Never had she been happier or more content.

The glow didn't last past morning. They'd made love again during the night, and Vanessa had begun to feel as if she never wanted to leave. To heck with everything else.

But she had a job, and Tim hadn't asked her to stay. Even as they were eating breakfast, the loss began to creep into her bones. She should have known better.

"Vanessa? Are you okay?"

She summoned a smile. "Never better. Last night was…incredible."

He smiled, but she suspected he didn't quite believe her. Her demons had returned.

She was saved, if she could call it that, but a phone call from work. It was the director of paleontology at the museum.

"I know you're on vacation, but can you finish it a little later? We need you back. On Friday we got a whole new shipment of bones—they seem to be from a very rare species, and they desperately need preservation and identification. Unfortunately, Carla was in an auto accident last night and won't be back for weeks or months, so we're down a hand, and we can't afford it. You're the best at identification anyway. Can you get back immediately? I'll make it up to you."

When she hung up, she looked at Tim and felt a crack begin to creep through her heart. "You'll never believe an emergency in a paleontology lab, but we've got one. One of my coworkers was in an accident, and they have a shipment of important bones that need preservation and identification. I've got to go back."

Tim grew very still. "When?"

"I need to arrange a flight today. I'll probably need to leave as soon as I pack." The crack in her heart grew more painful. "I need to call Ashley, too. I'll tell her I'll be back as soon as I can to talk to her class."

"It's that urgent?" His tone sounded tense.

"I'm sorry, but yes."

He nodded. "I'll get Matthew back here before you leave so you can say goodbye."

"Thank you."

She rose, breakfast forgotten, and went to her room, where she began to arrange a flight while she packed. Impossible, she supposed, to explain to anyone why this request from the director couldn't wait. The fossils had been waiting for millennia. Why couldn't they wait for a few weeks?

Because they were already rotting from exposure to the air and bacteria. Because time really *was* of the essence. Because the museum had a grant to do this kind of work, and failing to do it could cost them future grants. She got it. She doubted anyone else would. And from the director's perspective, did it matter if she took her vacation in a couple of months?

Of course not. And it shouldn't matter to her, either. But it did.

Chapter Eleven

A little over two months later, with Thanksgiving in the rearview and Christmas just ahead, Tim and Matthew waited impatiently for Vanessa's return.

She'd been talking to them on Skype, and Matthew treasured the postcards she sent—all from the museum's gift shop, evidently. He'd kept asking when she'd come again, and now, at last, she was.

Finally her rental car pulled up in front of the house. It was a frigid night. Snow covered the ground. That didn't keep Matthew from running out—without a jacket, in his regular shoes—to greet her. She hardly got out of the car before he leaped at her. She surprised Tim by catching the boy and holding him as she walked toward the house.

Despite all their conversations, Tim moved more

slowly, unsure what to expect. He'd finished most of the major work on the house and was looking forward to showing her. He was also ready to argue again that she should sell it to him.

But mostly he was glad to have her back. To have her home. When they met on the sidewalk, he embraced her and his son as best he could and managed to drop a kiss on her lips.

"Welcome home," he said, not caring if it was a bad choice of words.

"I'm so happy to be back." Her face reflected her words, so different from when she'd first arrived and had looked ready for trouble. Now nothing but smiles.

Inside he had hot coffee, some sweet rolls from the bakery and a mug of chocolate for Matthew, who yammered a mile a minute and finally spoke a truth that resonated to Tim's core. "I missed you, Vannie," the boy said. "I wish you didn't ever have to go away again."

Tim's and Vanessa's eyes met over the boy's head. Uncertainty. He saw her uncertainty. What about?

"We've already had dinner," he said, feeling awkward. "But I can make you something."

She shook her head. "I ate earlier. I'm fine."

"Come see my dinosaurs," Matthew said, tugging her hand. "I want you to see them."

She'd already seen the completed models on Skype, but she still smiled and followed him to the dining room, where the models had pride of place on the big table.

"Wow, you did a perfect job! I guess I need to get you some more."

"They make more?" Matthew's face lit up. "I want to be a palee...palo..."

"Paleontologist," she supplied gently.

"Yeah, like you. Except I want to dig up the bones."

"You'll get a chance to try it out," she said. "I'm going to be leading a dig not far from here come spring."

Tim's heart nearly stopped. "I thought you liked the museum."

"I do. But the museum is funding this with donations, and I got tapped to lead. Some hiker from New Mexico found something really interesting, and he sent the photos to us. Permissions are still being worked out, and we'll be cooperating with local universities. But yeah, in the spring I'll be digging again, and Matthew's welcome to come try his hand. It looks like a spectacular find."

Tim was still wrestling with the idea of Vannie being so close from spring to fall and wondering why she had decided to return to work she'd left behind.

Questions he couldn't ask until Matthew was in bed. The hands on the clock seemed to be dragging.

As happy as Vanessa was to see Matthew again, she was even happier to see Tim. Except he seemed subdued, and she wondered if she'd done something wrong. When he came down from putting Matthew to bed, she had to ask.

"Did I make a mistake by coming?"

He looked surprised. "Hell, no. What makes you think that?"

"You're being too quiet." She felt her insides congealing. Had she made a mistake? Had she put herself in a position to be hurt yet again?

He drew her into the living room and sat beside her on the couch. "I'm thrilled to see you. As thrilled as

Matthew is. You said you don't like digging. Why are you going back to it?"

She bit her lip, tensing until she might snap, feeling as if she were about to open herself to the biggest pain possible. "Because... I want to be near you."

His eyes narrowed. "Seriously?"

"Seriously."

"Wow," he murmured. "I didn't dare... I couldn't hope..."

The next thing she knew, he'd lifted her onto his lap and kissed her so deeply she lost her breath. When he tore his mouth away, he asked, "Just how close do you want to be?"

She hesitated then admitted, "As close as you want me. As long as you want me."

She watched his face change. The last tension seeped out of it. He closed his eyes and said quietly, "I want you close, and forever might just about do it."

Her heart began to lift, the last of her fears scattered to the winds. "How close is close?"

"Like...married?"

"I'll only be here part of the year."

"I'll take whatever part I can get. I love you, Vannie. I'm ready to move on. Are you?"

She never hesitated. "Oh, yes. Yes, yes, yes. Forever."

He smiled and squeezed her until she squeaked.

All of a sudden Matthew's voice interrupted them. "So Vannie's going to be my new mom?" He sounded excited.

"Do you want me?" she asked.

He climbed right on her lap as she sat on his father's

lap. "Yup. I can go camping at the dig, right? And you'll be here in the summers, right? And I can dig up bones?"

Vanessa looked at Tim over his head, and they both started laughing.

"Yes, yes, yes," she said again. "To both of you."

It had been a strange courtship in some ways. She'd hardly been aware it was happening. But now she had a family again. A real, beautiful family.

Her heart soared, and she hugged the two men she loved most in the world.

She had never believed she would know this kind of happiness, yet now it showered her. She would hang on to it with all her might. Forever.

* * * * *

Julia Winston is looking to conquer life, not become heartbreaker Jamie Caine's latest conquest. But when two young brothers wind up in Julia's care for the holidays, she'll take any help she can get—even Jamie's.

Read on for a preview of
New York Times *bestselling author*
RaeAnne Thayne's
SUGAR PINE TRAIL,
the latest installment in her beloved
HAVEN POINT *series.*

CHAPTER ONE

THIS WAS GOING to be a disaster.

Julia Winston stood in her front room looking out the lace curtains framing her bay window at the gleaming black SUV parked in her driveway like a sleek, predatory beast.

Her stomach jumped with nerves, and she rubbed suddenly clammy hands down her skirt. Under what crazy moon had she ever thought this might be a good idea? She must have been temporarily out of her head.

Those nerves jumped into overtime when a man stepped out of the vehicle and stood for a moment, looking up at her house.

Jamie Caine.

Tall, lean, hungry.

Gorgeous.

Now the nerves felt more like nausea. What had she done? The moment Eliza Caine called and asked her if her brother-in-law could rent the upstairs apartment of Winston House, she should have told her friend in no uncertain terms that the idea was preposterous. Utterly impossible.

As usual, Julia had been weak and indecisive, and when Eliza told her it was only for six weeks—until January, when the condominium Jamie Caine was buying in

a new development along the lake would be finished—
she had wavered.

He needed a place to live, and she *did* need the
money. Anyway, it was only for six weeks. Surely she
could tolerate having the man living upstairs in her
apartment for six weeks—especially since he would be
out of town for much of those six weeks as part of his
duties as lead pilot for the Caine Tech company jet fleet.

The reality of it all was just beginning to sink in,
though. Jamie Caine, upstairs from her, in all his sexy,
masculine glory.

She fanned herself with her hand, wondering if she
was having a premature-onset hot flash or if her new
furnace could be on the fritz. The temperature in here
seemed suddenly off the charts.

How would she tolerate having him here, spending
her evenings knowing he was only a few steps away and
that she would have to do her best to hide the absolutely
ridiculous, truly humiliating crush she had on the man?

This was such a mistake.

Heart pounding, she watched through the frothy curtains as he pulled a long black duffel bag from the back
of his SUV and slung it over his shoulder, lifted a laptop case over the other shoulder, then closed the cargo
door and headed for the front steps.

A moment later, her old-fashioned musical doorbell
echoed through the house. If she hadn't been so nervous, she might have laughed at the instant reaction of
the three cats, previously lounging in various states of
boredom around the room. The moment the doorbell
rang, Empress and Tabitha both jumped off the sofa as if

an electric current had just zipped through it, while Audrey Hepburn arched her back and bushed out her tail.

"That's right, girls. We've got company. It's a man, believe it or not, and he's moving in upstairs. Get ready."

The cats sniffed at her with their usual disdainful look. Empress ran in front of her, almost tripping her on the way to answer the door—on purpose, she was quite sure.

With her mother's cats darting out ahead of her, Julia walked out into what used to be the foyer of the house before she had created the upstairs apartment and now served as an entryway to both residences. She opened the front door, doing her best to ignore the rapid tripping of her heartbeat.

"Hi. You're Julia, right?"

As his sister-in-law was one of her dearest friends, she and Jamie had met numerous times at various events at Snow Angel Cove and elsewhere, but she didn't bother reminding him of that. Julia knew she was eminently forgettable. Most of the time, that was just the way she liked it.

"Yes. Hello, Mr. Caine."

He aimed his high-wattage killer smile at her. "Please. Jamie. Nobody calls me Mr. Caine."

Julia was grimly aware of her pulse pounding in her ears and a strange hitch in her lungs. Up close, Jamie Caine was, in a word, breathtaking. He was Mr. Darcy, Atticus Finch, Rhett Butler and Tom Cruise in *Top Gun* all rolled into one glorious package.

Dark hair, blue eyes and that utterly charming Caine smile he shared with Aidan, Eliza's husband, and the other Caine brothers she had met at various events.

"You were expecting me, right?" he said after an awkward pause. She jolted, suddenly aware she was staring and had left him standing entirely too long on her front step. She was an idiot. "Yes. Of course. Come in. I'm sorry."

Pull yourself together. He's just a guy who happens to be gorgeous.

So far she was seriously failing at Landlady 101. She sucked in a breath and summoned her most brisk keep-your-voice-down-please librarian persona.

"As you can see, we will share the entry. Because the home is on the registry of historical buildings, I couldn't put in an outside entrance to your apartment, as I might have preferred. The house was built in 1880, one of the earliest brick homes on Lake Haven. It was constructed by an ancestor of mine, Sir Robert Winston, who came from a wealthy British family and made his own fortune supplying timber to the railroads. He also invested in one of the first hot-springs resorts in the area. The home is Victorian, specifically in the spindled Queen Anne style. It consists of seven bedrooms and four bathrooms. When those bathrooms were added in the 1920s, they provided some of the first indoor plumbing in the region."

"Interesting," he said, though his expression indicated he found it anything but.

She was rambling, she realized, as she tended to do when she was nervous.

She cleared her throat and pointed to the doorway, where the three cats were lined up like sentinels, watching him with unblinking stares. "Anyway, through those doors is my apartment and yours is upstairs. I have keys to both doors for you along with a packet of information here."

She glanced toward the ornate marble-top table in the entryway—that her mother claimed once graced the mansion of Leland Stanford on Nob Hill in San Francisco—where she thought she had left the information. Unfortunately, it was bare. "Oh. Where did I put that? I must have left it inside in my living room. Just a moment."

The cats weren't inclined to get out of her way, so she stepped over them, wondering if she came across as eccentric to him as she felt, a spinster librarian living with cats in a crumbling house crammed with antiques, a space much too big for one person.

After a mad scan of the room, she finally found the two keys along with the carefully prepared file folder of instructions atop the mantel, nestled amid her collection of porcelain angels. She had no recollection of moving them there, probably due to her own nervousness at having Jamie Caine moving upstairs.

She swooped them up and hurried back to the entry, where she found two of the cats curled around his leg, while Audrey was in his arms, currently being petted by his long, square-tipped fingers.

She stared. The cats had no time or interest in her. She only kept them around because her mother had adored them, and Julia couldn't bring herself to give away Mariah's adored pets. Apparently no female—human or feline—was immune to Jamie Caine. She should have expected it.

"Nice cats."

Julia frowned. "Not usually. They're standoffish and bad tempered to most people."

"I guess I must have the magic touch."

So the Haven Point rumor mill said about him, anyway. "I guess you do," she said. "I found your keys and information about the apartment. If you would like, I can show you around upstairs."

"Lead on."

He offered a friendly smile, and she told herself that shiver rippling down her spine was only because the entryway was cooler than her rooms.

"This is a lovely house," he said as he followed her up the staircase. "Have you lived here long?"

"Thirty-two years in February. All my life, in other words."

Except the first few days, anyway, when she had still been in the Oregon hospital where her parents adopted her, and the three years she had spent at Boise State.

"It's always been in my family," she continued. "My father was born here and his father before him."

She was a Winston only by adoption but claimed her parents' family trees as her own and respected and admired their ancestors and the elegant home they had built here.

At the second-floor landing, she unlocked the apartment that had been hers until she moved down to take care of her mother after Mariah's first stroke, two years ago. A few years after taking the job at the Haven Point library, she had redecorated the upstairs floor of the house. It had been her way of carving out her own space.

Yes, she had been an adult living with her parents. Even as she might have longed for some degree of independence, she couldn't justify moving out when her mother had so desperately needed her help with Julia's ailing father.

Anyway, she had always figured it wasn't the same as most young adults who lived in their parents' apartments. She'd had an entire self-contained floor to herself. If she wished, she could shop on her own, cook on her own, entertain her friends, all without bothering her parents.

Really, it had been the best of all situations—close enough to help, yet removed enough to live her own life. Then her father died and her mother became frail herself, and Julia had felt obligated to move downstairs to be closer, in case her mother needed her.

Now, as she looked at her once-cherished apartment, she tried to imagine how Jamie Caine would see these rooms, with the graceful reproduction furniture and the pastel wall colors and the soft carpet and curtains.

Oddly, the feminine decorations only served to emphasize how very *male* Jamie Caine was, in contrast.

She did her best to ignore that unwanted observation.

"This is basically the same floor plan as my rooms below, with three bedrooms, as well as the living room and kitchen," she explained. "You've got an en suite bathroom off the largest bedroom and another one for the other two bedrooms."

"Wow. That's a lot of room for one guy."

"It's a big house," she said with a shrug. She had even more room downstairs, factoring in the extra bedroom in one addition and the large south-facing sunroom.

Winston House was entirely too rambling for one single woman and three bad-tempered cats. It had been too big for an older couple and their adopted daughter. It had been too large when it was just her and her mother, after her father died.

The place had basically echoed with emptiness for the better part of a year after her mother's deteriorating condition had necessitated her move to the nursing home in Shelter Springs. Her mother had hoped to return to the house she had loved, but that never happened, and Mariah Winston died four months ago.

Julia missed her every single day.

"Do you think it will work for you?" she asked.

"It's more than I need, but should be fine. Eliza told you this is only temporary, right?"

Julia nodded. She was counting on it. Then she could find a nice, quiet, older lady to rent who wouldn't leave her so nervous.

"She said your apartment lease ran out before your new condo was finished."

"Yes. The development was supposed to be done two months ago, but the builder has suffered delay after delay. I've already extended my lease twice. I didn't want to push my luck with my previous landlady by asking for a third extension."

All Jamie had to do was smile at the woman and she likely would have extended his lease again without quibbling. And probably would have given him anything else he wanted, too.

Julia didn't ask why he chose not to move into Snow Angel Cove with his brother Aidan and Aidan's wife, Eliza, and their children. It was none of her business, anyway. The only thing she cared about was the healthy amount he was paying her in rent, which would just about cover the new furnace she had installed a month earlier.

"It was a lucky break for me when Eliza told me you were considering taking on a renter for your upstairs space."

He aimed that killer smile at her again, and her core muscles trembled from more than just her workout that morning.

If she wasn't very, very careful, she would end up making a fool of herself over the man.

It took effort, but she fought the urge to return his smile. This was business, she told herself. That was all. She had something he needed, a place to stay, and he was willing to pay for it. She, in turn, needed funds if she wanted to maintain this house that had been in her family for generations.

"It works out for both of us. You've already signed the rental agreement outlining the terms of your tenancy and the rules."

She held out the information packet. "Here you'll find all the information you might need, information like internet access, how to work the electronics and the satellite television channels, garbage pickup day and mail delivery. Do you have any other questions?"

Business, she reminded herself, making her voice as no-nonsense and brisk as possible.

"I can't think of any now, but I'm sure something will come up."

He smiled again, but she thought perhaps this time his expression was a little more reserved. Maybe he could sense she was un-charmable.

Or so she wanted to tell herself, anyway.

"I would ask that you please wipe your feet when you carry your things in and out, given the snow out there. The stairs are original wood, more than a hundred years old."

Cripes. She sounded like a prissy spinster librarian.

"I will do that, but I don't have much to carry in. Since El told me the place is furnished, I put almost everything in storage." He gestured to the duffel and laptop bag, which he had set inside the doorway. "Besides this, I've only got a few more boxes in the car."

"In that case, here are your keys. The large one goes to the outside door. The smaller one is for your apartment. I keep the outside door locked at all times. You can't be too careful."

"True enough."

She glanced at her watch. "I'm afraid I've already gone twenty minutes past my lunch hour and must return to the library. My cell number is written on the front of the packet, in case of emergency."

"Looks like you've covered everything."

"I think so." Yes, she was a bit obsessively organized, and she didn't like surprises. Was anything wrong with that?

"I hope you will be comfortable here," she said, then tried to soften her stiff tone with a smile that felt every bit as awkward. "Good afternoon."

"Uh, same to you."

Her heart was still pounding as she nodded to him and hurried for the stairs, desperate for escape from all that…masculinity.

She rushed back downstairs and into her apartment

for her purse, wishing she had time to splash cold water on her face.

However would she get through the next six weeks with him in her house?

He was *not* looking forward to the next six weeks.

Jamie stood in the corner of the main living space to the apartment he had agreed to rent, sight unseen.

Big mistake.

It was roomy and filled with light, that much was true. But the decor was too…fussy…for a man like him, all carved wood and tufted upholstery and pastel wall colorings.

It wasn't exactly his scene, more like the kind of place a repressed, uppity librarian might live.

As soon as he thought the words, Jamie frowned at himself. That wasn't fair. She might not have been overflowing with warmth and welcome, but Julia Winston had been very polite to him—especially since he knew she hadn't necessarily wanted to rent to him.

This was what happened when he gave his sister-in-law free rein to find him an apartment in the tight local rental market. She had been helping him out, since he had been crazy busy the last few weeks flying Caine Tech execs from coast to coast—and all places in between—as they worked on a couple of big mergers.

Eliza had wanted him to stay at her and Aidan's rambling house by the lake. The place was huge, and they had plenty of room, but while he loved his older brother Aidan and his wife and kids, Jamie preferred his own space. He didn't much care what that space looked like, especially when it was temporary.

With time running out on his lease extension, he had been relieved when Eliza called him via Skype the week before to tell him she had found him something more than suitable, for a decent rent.

"You'll love it!" Eliza had beamed. "It's the entire second floor of a gorgeous old Victorian in that great neighborhood on Snow Blossom Lane, with a simply stunning view of the lake."

"Sounds good," he had answered.

"You'll be upstairs from my friend Julia Winston, and, believe me, you couldn't ask for a better land-lady. She's sweet and kind and perfectly wonderful. You know Julia, right?"

When he had looked blankly at her and didn't immediately respond, his niece Maddie had popped her face into the screen from where she had been apparently listening in off camera. "You know! She's the library lady. She tells all the stories!"

"Ah. *That* Julia," he'd said, not bothering to mention to his seven-year-old niece that in more than a year of living in town, he had somehow missed out on story time at the Haven Point library.

He also didn't mention to Maddie's mother that he only vaguely remembered Julia Winston. Now that he had seen her again, he understood why. She was the kind of woman who tended to slip into the background—and he had the odd impression that wasn't accidental.

She wore her brown hair past her shoulders, with-out much curl or style to it and held back with a simple black band, and she appeared to use little makeup to play up her rather average features.

She did have lovely eyes, he had to admit. Extraordinary, even. They were a stunning blue, almost violet, fringed by naturally long eyelashes.

Her looks didn't matter, nor did the decor of her house. He would only be here a few weeks, then he would be moving into his new condo.

She clearly didn't like him. He frowned, wondering how he might have offended Julia Winston. He barely remembered even meeting the woman, but he must have done something for her to be so cool to him.

A few times during that odd interaction, she had alternated between seeming nervous to be in the same room with him to looking at him with her mouth pursed tightly, as if she had just caught him spreading peanut butter across the pages of *War and Peace*.

She was entitled to her opinion. Contrary to popular belief, he didn't need everyone to like him.

His brothers would probably say it was good for him to live upstairs from a woman so clearly immune to his charm.

One thing was clear: he now had one more reason to be eager for his condo to be finished.

Don't miss SUGAR PINE TRAIL
by RaeAnne Thayne
Available October 2017 from HQN Books!

SPECIAL EXCERPT FROM

HARLEQUIN®

SPECIAL EDITION
TM

*Ella Baker is trading music lessons for riding
lessons from the wild twin McKinley boys—but it's
their father who would need a Christmas miracle to
let Ella into his heart.*

*Read on for a sneak preview of
the RANCHER'S CHRISTMAS SONG,
the next book in* New York Times *bestselling author
RaeAnne Thayne's beloved miniseries
THE COWBOYS OF COLD CREEK.*

Beckett finally spoke. "Uh, what seems to be the trouble?"

His voice had an odd, strangled note to it. Was he laughing at her? When she couldn't see him, Ella couldn't be quite sure. "It's stuck in my hair comb. I don't want to rip the sweater—or yank out my hair, for that matter."

He paused again, then she felt the air stir as he moved closer. The scent of him was stronger now, masculine and outdoorsy, and everything inside her sighed a welcome.

He stood close enough that she could feel the heat radiating from him. She caught her breath, torn between a completely prurient desire for the moment to last at least a little longer and a wild hope that the humiliation of being caught in this position would be over quickly.

"Hold still," he said. Was his voice deeper than usual? She couldn't quite tell. She did know it sent tiny delicious shivers down her spine.

"You've really done a job here," he said after a moment.

"I know. I'm not quite sure how it tangled so badly."

She would have to breathe soon or she was likely to pass out. She forced herself to inhale one breath and then another until she felt a little less light-headed.

"Almost there," he said, his big hands in her hair, then a moment later she felt a tug and the sweater slipped all the way over her head.

"There you go."

"Thank you." She wanted to disappear, to dive under that great big log bed and hide away. Instead, she forced her mouth into a casual smile. "These Christmas sweaters can be dangerous. Who knew?"

She was blushing. She could feel her face heat and wondered if he noticed. This certainly counted among the most embarrassing moments of her life.

"Want to explain again what you're doing in my bedroom, tangled up in your clothes?" he asked.

She frowned at his deliberately risqué interpretation of something that had been innocent. Mostly.

There had been that secret moment when she had closed her eyes and imagined being here with him under that soft quilt, but he had no way of knowing that.

She folded up her sweater, wondering if she would ever be able to look the man in the eye again.

Don't miss
THE RANCHER'S CHRISTMAS SONG
by RaeAnne Thayne,
available November 2017 wherever
Harlequin® Special Edition books and ebooks are sold.

www.Harlequin.com

$7.99 U.S./$9.99 CAN.

EXCLUSIVE
Limited Time Offer

$1.⁰⁰ OFF

New York Times Bestselling Author

RaeAnne Thayne

SUGAR PINE TRAIL

*An unlikely attraction brings comfort, joy and
unforgettable romance this holiday season!*

*Available September 26, 2017.
Pick up your copy today!*

HQN™

$1.⁰⁰
OFF

the purchase price of SUGAR PINE TRAIL
by RaeAnne Thayne.

Offer valid from September 26, 2017 to October 31, 2017.
Redeemable at participating retail outlets. Not redeemable at Barnes & Noble.
Limit one coupon per purchase. Valid in the U.S.A. and Canada only.

52615030

Canadian Retailers: Harlequin Enterprises Limited will pay the face value of this coupon plus 10.25¢ if submitted by customer for this product only. Any other use constitutes fraud. Coupon is nonassignable. Void if taxed, prohibited or restricted by law. Consumer must pay any government taxes. Void if copied. Inmar Promotional Services ("IPS") customers submit coupons and proof of sales to Harlequin Enterprises Limited, P.O. Box 31000, Scarborough, ON M1R 0E7, Canada. Non-IPS retailer—for reimbursement submit coupons and proof of sales directly to Harlequin Enterprises Limited, Retail Marketing Department, 225 Duncan Mill Rd., Don Mills, ON M3B 3K9, Canada.

U.S. Retailers: Harlequin Enterprises Limited will pay the face value of this coupon plus 8¢ if submitted by customer for this product only. Any other use constitutes fraud. Coupon is nonassignable. Void if taxed, prohibited or restricted by law. Consumer must pay any government taxes. Void if copied. For reimbursement submit coupons and proof of sales directly to Harlequin Enterprises, Ltd 482, NCH Marketing Services, P.O. Box 880001, El Paso, TX 88588-0001, U.S.A. Cash value 1/100 cents

5 65373 00076 2 (8100)0 12300

® and ™ are trademarks owned and used by the trademark owner and/or its licensee.

© 2017 Harlequin Enterprises Limited

PHCOUPRATSE1017

Looking for more satisfying love stories
with community and family at their core?

**Check out Harlequin® Special Edition
and Harlequin® Western Romance books!**

New books available every month!

CONNECT WITH US AT:

Harlequin.com/Community

 Facebook.com/HarlequinBooks

Twitter.com/HarlequinBooks

Instagram.com/HarlequinBooks

Pinterest.com/HarlequinBooks

ReaderService.com

**ROMANCE WHEN
YOU NEED IT**

THE WORLD IS BETTER WITH

Romance

Harlequin has everything from contemporary, passionate and heartwarming to suspenseful and inspirational stories.

Whatever your mood, we have a romance just for you!

Connect with us to find your next great read, special offers and more.

f /HarlequinBooks

🐦 @HarlequinBooks

www.HarlequinBlog.com

www.Harlequin.com/Newsletters

HARLEQUIN®

A *Romance* FOR EVERY MOOD™

www.Harlequin.com